to S...

MADDIE MARZOLA

First Alien

Maddie
Marzola
S

First published by Bonafide Publishing 2023

First edition

This book was professionally typeset on Reedsy.
Find out more at reedsy.com

To my sister
I wish you were here
The way I wish I was there

The air didn't smell right. The musky scent of the trees was there, as was the earthy undertone of the damp ground, but it was all dulled by a tasteless extra layer. The woods shouldn't smell like that.

In Lucy's list of complaints, however, that was barely in the top five. Her boyfriend Matthew's idea of a fun hike in the Forest of Dean had already presented her with cold, hunger, and a generous amount of pain at the back of her right heel. It all was made even worse by the daunting awareness that whatever distance she hiked forwards, she'd have to hike back.

Even Frank hadn't been too convinced about going in the woods on a muggy November day, despite his general enthusiasm for whatever Matthew suggested. Looking at him, Lucy sometimes wondered if it shouldn't be her brother dating Matthew after all. It had become an inside joke.

Leaning against a tree to catch her breath, Lucy looked ahead. Frank was waiting for her by a giant oak tree. "Are you alright back there?"

Not surprisingly, it was her brother who turned to check on her. After her powerful morning display of passive aggressiveness, Matthew was keeping his distance. She could barely spot him further ahead amongst the fir trees, a smudge of red waterproof fabric amidst the grey hue of the woods on that muggy day.

She still wasn't going to apologise. She was never going to fall in love with hiking boots and muddy trails just because her boyfriend's mum had suddenly shown up with a tip on a new trail in the Wye Valley – and she still thought it was rather odd how insistent Mrs Cavell had been about them going that very weekend.

"Is there a reward at the end of this pain or is he leading us to starvation?" she asked as she joined her brother and leaned heavily against the oak trunk.

He raised an eyebrow in amusement. "Are you asking for a piggy ride?"

Lucy glared at him. "Fuck you," she said, raising her favourite finger, lest he misunderstood her tone.

He laughed at that, and she couldn't hold back a smile herself. Then Frank's grin waned, and he cocked his head in that condescending way of his. "Seriously, though, we can stop for a bit, if you need to rest."

How she hated that tone. "Frank, I can walk."

He turned away, hands thrown high in a gesture of surrender, but she could still see his eyes rolling.

Annoying tone aside, she was glad he had agreed to join them. He was a buffering force to Matthew's sulky mood.

Then he tilted his head up, sniffing the air. "Do you smell that?"

"I know, it's weird."

"Maybe somebody's having a bonfire somewhere nearby," he guessed.

"Why would you think it's a bonfire?"

"Because it smells like burning, and bonfires are famous for

2

that." His smirk was infuriating.

She limited her reaction to a dull gaze. "I'm humbled by your superior wisdom, milord."

He was about to reply when something else caught his attention. Further up the path, Matthew had stopped walking. Standing a few feet off the track, he was gazing at something in the distance. Lucy squinted to catch what it was and for a second the odd scent felt a bit stronger, as if electricity was burning up her nostrils. As if a storm was coming and they were walking amongst the charged clouds. It made her want to sneeze.

Past Matthew, something large and dark nested amongst the trees.

Ignoring the persisting pain up her calves, Lucy scurried forward until she reached the edge of the clearing. Even from there, it didn't look like anything she'd seen before, starting from the colour – a shade of black that wanted to absorb all the light around it, so much so that a halo of darkness seemed to envelop the whole thing.

The metal structure – because it had to be some kind of metal – took up most of the space, and it seemed to have knocked down a few trees as well, as if it had crashed into them while parking itself there. Something that looked like a wing spread out from a thicker and rounder main body. Aside from that, there was no other indication of what it might be.

"What the hell is that?" she managed, while her brain kept on processing.

"Holy moly," whispered Frank as he stepped next to her.

She glanced sideways at him. "Frankie, your non-swearing attitude is getting ridiculous. This is clearly a *holy fuck* kind of moment."

3

The only one of them to remain nonplussed seemed to be Matthew. "There's a few old and new RAF bases in the region," he said as he walked up to their side. "This is probably one of their prototypes. It must have gotten lost in the woods."

"Because *that* sounds likely," commented Lucy.

"Do you have a better explanation?"

"Better than the army losing their new toy in the middle of a national park? Yes, I think I can come up with something."

Before Matthew could retort, Frank jumped in between them. "Who wants to go and have a look?"

Bless his heart – or his scientific curiosity, as he liked to call it. Give him a weird shiny trinket in the middle of the woods, and Frank would revert to the recklessness of a six-year-old on a sugar rush, to the point where Lucy had to be the sensible one getting him out of trouble. Given that she was the one with a criminal record, the irony of that wasn't lost on anybody.

Matthew, on the other hand, wasn't keen on running towards the flame. "I don't think so. Better stay away and call the authorities on this one. It's clearly none of our business."

Lucy gave him a condescending look. "Are you scared of meeting the little green passengers?"

"Luce, this doesn't look like a joke. It might be dangerous."

Once again, Frank stepped in to quell the argument and rested a hand on Matthew's shoulder. "Ten minutes," he pleaded.

Lucy grinned at him, in spite of everything. She wasn't excited about following him into a mysterious and quite certainly dangerous metal container. "Yeah, ten minutes," she said, then turned to Matthew. "Fifteen tops, then I'll bring the baby back to the pram, and you can go ahead and call James Bond to examine the relic."

Frank was already a few steps ahead, waiting for Lucy to join.

Matthew sighed. "No way to stop him, is there?"

"You know him. Not a chance."

She rushed to join her brother, spikes of pain forcing her to slow her pace as she got closer. She was really going to feel it the next day, she thought. She leaned on Frank once she was close enough.

"You really should stop hopping around like that," he scolded her.

"I don't know what you're talking about."

"Are you going to be okay walking back?"

She shrugged. "Unless we fly this thing out of here, I'll have to."

As they walked closer, they tried to stay clear of the overhanging wing-shaped structure, the electricity in the air around them getting stronger, much like how the light of day seemed to be getting dimmer.

When Lucy reached out a hand to touch the metallic surface, she almost expected to get zapped by an electric discharge. She didn't. It felt warm to the touch.

A layer of dirt covered it. She wiped some off with her hand, then stared at her darkened reflection on the shiny material.

"Have you ever seen anything like this?" she asked. Her voice came out muffled, the air as thick as cotton candy as she spoke. She turned to Frank, worried he might not have heard her at all. "We should probably go back," she said, a bit louder this time. "I have a bad feeling about this." Her own voice sounded like it was coming from miles away.

Frank scoffed. "Calm your nerves, Han. It's not like we're looking at an actual spaceship."

It would have been a funny Star Wars reference, if Han Solo's instinct hadn't been so good at spotting life-threatening danger.

She took a step back, wondering if she was overreacting, and if the Royal Air Force could really have lost something like this and left it to dust. The surface looked smooth from end to end, a master-size metal origami.

"Luce, come look at this."

When she turned, Frank was standing so close to the surface, his nose was almost brushing against it.

"Have you thought it might be better not to stick your nose in the shiny thing?" she reproached him.

"Yeah, but this is interesting. Come look." He cocked his head and brushed his thumb against it. "It's like a panel or something."

He picked at it with his fingernails, trying to tear it open, but it was no use.

"Let me see," she said, giving him a slight shove.

He moved aside to make room for her.

The gap was maybe a millimetre wide, barely visible. She ran a finger alongside it, then swung her backpack forward to get her keys out.

"What are you doing?" asked Frank.

"Trying to get this over with, so we can get out of here."

"I mean with the keys."

"Oh, that. Leverage – you heard of it?" she replied. "And here was me thinking you were good at science."

"You think too highly of me," he joked. "I do chemistry, remember? No need for leverage when you're distilling vodka from potatoes."

She picked the smallest and pointiest key, the one to lock the chain of the bike she never used, and started working at the gap, blushing slightly at the pink sloth keyring dangling by her

6

wrist. The colour was faded after years spent in Lucy's pocket, but the flash drive still worked. It was filled with videos and photos of her childhood, carefully curated by her brother, and gifted to her the night before she left home and never spoke to her parents again. Since then, that well-worn plush toy had been her most valuable possession.

"You're still carrying that around," said Frank, noticing the pink fluff.

Lucy shrugged it off. Then, before she could say anything, something went *click* somewhere behind the panel, which slid aside, opening a square-foot gap into nothing.

She jerked away, holding her hands up. Hairs rose on the back of her neck. "I didn't do that."

Frank peered at the dark opening. For him, Christmas had arrived early. "Maybe you hit a switch or something."

"I don't like this, Frankie," she whispered.

They held their breath, and it seemed the woods did too, as if waiting for something to crawl out of the open panel.

Seconds passed, however, and nothing happened, yet Lucy could sense something was waiting just around the corner.

She took a couple of steps back and checked on Matthew. He was facing the other way, probably on the phone with the police. How odd that she couldn't hear a word he was saying. Sounds carried differently in the woods, she knew that, but she was sure they weren't standing that far apart.

The sound of feet shuffling by her side startled her – there was still sound in the world, then. Frank had moved closer to the small dark window and was trying to peer inside.

"Frank," she said, her voice hollow in the padded air. She should have pulled him away, yet she found she couldn't move. She saw him squinting at something, then leaning closer.

7

"What is it?"

"I'm sure there's something down there," he said, as he grabbed the edge of the opening. He looked ready to jump inside.

"Don't do anything stupid. Whatever it is, it might be dangerous." She felt it was.

Frank stepped back with a chuckle, then turned towards her. "You've seen way too many alien films, you know?"

And you haven't seen enough, she thought. "Still, you don't know what's in there."

He gave her a cocky smirk. "Precisely. Mine is scientific curiosity."

There it was again, his favourite line. Even Lucy's scoff was half-hearted. "We should get back. Matt's already called the men in black."

She made to leave, but Frank was once again staring into the dark gap.

Something was going to happen, she could feel it. Part of her wouldn't have been surprised to see Frank hit by a laser beam, or teleported to a galaxy far, far away.

She swallowed her fear. "What's wrong, Frankie?"

His response was somewhat absent. "I don't know."

Then it happened.

A flash.

A blink-and-you-miss-it sort of event.

Something had shot out of the opening and straight into Frank's jacket. Lucy shrieked and stepped away, ending up flat against the metal wall behind her.

Frank had bolted away from the opening as well – one springing step – and was now standing still, as if he had forgotten what had made him jump in the first place.

Matthew's voice reached them from another world on the edge of the clearing. "Guys, is everything okay? What happened?"

Lucy waved at him, opened her mouth, but didn't say anything. She had no idea how to answer the question.

"Help is on the way!" he shouted. Bless him, he was trying to be reassuring.

She didn't know what to do. If she raised the alarm and Matthew rushed down to help, he'd be in just as much danger as Lucy and Frank were.

Eventually, she raised her hand and gave him a thumbs-up. Then, under her breath: "Shit."

Frank still looked as if he had gone into standby mode, a videogame on pause, his gaze unfocussed and his arms hanging limp from his shoulders.

"Frank?" she tried. "Are you okay?"

He tilted his head upwards towards the sky, then lowered it to look at her. For a second, Lucy doubted he recognised her, until the whole system went back online. He gave her the fakest smile in the book and said, "Of course I'm okay. Never been better."

He was still breathing and talking, so that was a good sign. Whatever animal crept out of the hole didn't have to be bad news. *It could've been a squirrel*, she thought. *Please let it be a squirrel.*

"Matthew called the police. They'll be here any minute," she said.

The fake smile was still hanging on Frank's face. He looked okay, and at the same time as far from the shores of Okay Land as a man could be.

She stole another glance at Matthew, who was on the phone

once again and looking away from them. Lucy had never liked the police, a feeling she knew was reciprocated, yet this time she felt like throwing them a welcome party.

"I need more time."

She flinched at Frank's words. "What do you mean?" she asked, but he was again in standby mode, gaze unfocussed and chin down. Her brother was in front of her, yet it wasn't her brother looking through those eyes.

Whatever jumped onto him was still hidden somewhere in his jacket. She stepped forward and felt her firsts clenching as a wave of frustration gripped her throat. She was ready to punch whatever worm was crawling over her brother.

"Frank, what's going on?" she demanded, her voice shakier than she had expected it to be. "What do you need more time for?"

He shook his head slowly, methodically. "There's too much to learn. I need more time," he murmured.

"Frankie, this is not funny. You've managed to scare me, if that's what you wanted. Now, please stop."

"Why are you scared?" he asked.

"Because you're re-enacting a cheap horror film scene, that's why," she replied, her voice rising to a screech. She checked her nerves and tried again. "The police are almost here. They will have it all figured out. Just stop being creepy, okay?"

Her brother turned to glance at Matthew, and Lucy allowed herself a moment of optimism, until he spoke again. "Not the police," he said. "Does Frankie have a safe place to go? Can you take me there?"

The world stopped turning for a moment. Lucy felt her knees giving in. "Frankie? *You* are Frank. Are you?"

It couldn't possibly be, yet either Frank had lost his mind all of a sudden, or a mind-controlling squirrel had jumped out of a mysterious spaceship-looking structure and brainwashed him – or possessed him. No, that was crazy.

"What are you?" she asked. "How are you doing that – how are you talking through my brother?"

Another pause for thought – or whatever else was happening in Frank's head during that pause – then he said, "This body is not suited to pronounce the name of my kind, but you can call me Gwyn. My species are called Skaara. You wouldn't be familiar with our solar system, so I won't waste time explaining where that is."

Before she knew it, Lucy had stepped forward. "Don't you dare patronise me, you space leech," she burst out, reaching to grab her brother's jacket, eager to get a glimpse of the parasite and a chance to snatch it away.

It was her brother's arms that stopped her, as he gripped her wrists and kept her away. She had never realised he was so strong. "This body can easily overpower you," he said calmly. "I suggest you desist and cooperate."

She sure as hell wasn't going to desist. "Cooperate with what, you psycho?"

"Can you get me to Frank's safe place?" he repeated.

Lucy felt her eyes sting with warm tears. The cops couldn't arrive any faster. She straightened and snatched her hand out of Frank's grip. Bottling up her emotions, she said, "That depends. Can you explain to me what's happening, and what you're doing to my brother?"

The way Frank paused wasn't hesitation. He was calculating the options. Lucy could see it in his eyes, locked onto hers as if trying to read her mind. He even squinted a little, trying to read it better maybe. She allowed herself a smirk. "What, telepathy doesn't work at a distance?"

It was a wild guess, firmly belonging to the realm of science-fiction stories. When Frank didn't react to her words, she knew she hadn't hit far off the target.

Finally, he said, "Take me there, and I'll explain."

No, not yet. She took a step back and squared her feet, trying to convince herself she still had some control over the situation in spite of the lump in her throat. "No deal. Tell me what you've done to my brother, or I'm not taking you anywhere."

There was that stare again, drilling into her forehead, close to a physical assault, a violation of her space, as if hands were jutting out of his eyes and prying her mind open, one brain cell at a time. She turned away.

At the tree line, Matthew was looking at them. She waved again.

"What's the deal then?" she called out.

"They're sending a team," he confirmed. "They locked onto my GPS; they won't be long. Is your brother okay?"

His words came to her loud and clear, as if normality was restored, at least as far as sound was concerned. Lucy wasn't sure what that meant for Frank, though. When Lucy looked at him, he hadn't moved a muscle, gaze still locked on her. She turned back to Matthew, and once again didn't know how to answer his question.

No, he wasn't okay. He was being possessed by an alien critter that called itself Gwyn, of all names. He was far from okay.

"How long is a while?" asked Frank.

Lucy tried to ignore his gaze on her. "Don't know. Ten, fifteen minutes maybe." A wild exaggeration – or at least she hoped so. "What are you?" she then asked.

He pulled aside his unzipped jacket to show the grey hoody

underneath. A small, snake-like creature poked out of his armpit. It wasn't the whole thing, and Lucy wondered how much more of its body was hidden by the jacket.

"I wished so hard for you to be a squirrel," she murmured.

If he caught her words, he didn't catch her meaning. "I mean no harm," he said.

"Are you saying that with my brother's mouth?" Lucy scoffed. "You've got nerve."

Her hands itched to grab that thing away from Frank and rip it in half. She couldn't do that, though. Even if Frank's arms hadn't stopped her, she was too afraid to hurt him. Too afraid it would take control of her mind as well. Too afraid of becoming a puppet to some alien overlord, or even just an alien creeper.

"What are you doing to him?" she asked instead.

"He's fine, only tucked away. You don't have to worry about him."

"You'll have to elaborate on that."

The alien sighed through Frank's lips. "I'm only using him to communicate with you. Once I leave him, he will come back to himself."

"Plus the trauma of having a critter talking through his mouth."

Frank shook his head. "He won't remember anything."

There was still no sign of the police. She had to keep him talking, just for a little bit longer. "Why did you come to Earth? And how many of you are hidden in there anyway?"

Waving at the metal wall, she only realised she had stepped forward when Frank raised an arm to stop her. It was an odd gesture, as if the creature was testing how to move the puppet's limbs. "It's only me," he said. "Nobody else is in the vessel."

That didn't sound right. "An alien invasion of one?"

"Invasion," he muttered. "No, we don't use that word."

"What word would you use, then? Holiday? You should have landed in Florida; they've got Disneyland."

There were a couple of seconds of consideration, then he said, "No, that's beyond my area."

The alien's sense of humour was disappointing, yet that wasn't the most alarming part. "You mean another one is in the States? How many of you have landed?"

Whatever response he was planning to give was cut short as a distorted voice boomed out of a megaphone. "You two over there, don't move! Hold your hands up and turn your faces towards the wall."

The man was standing at the edge of the clearing, way too close to actually need a megaphone. A dozen more men were with him, weapons holstered, yet visibly ready to engage. Every one of them was dressed in black, and not one bothered identifying themselves. They didn't look like police, and it wasn't the army either, Lucy was sure.

She turned around, ready to do what they said, and by doing so noticed that Frank had barely reacted to the intromission, as if what was happening had nothing to do with him.

"You should do what they say, space genius," she told him.

"Those are contradicting orders," he commented.

Lucy threw her eyes to the sky. "Just raise your hands and turn around."

After a whole year out of trouble, it had taken a spaceship for Lucy to once again be in handcuffs. What a spectacular way to break such a good run.

After weeks out of town on a recon mission in the worst of weathers, Stephanie's desk at SafeOp Defence Services' headquarters looked to her like the most comfortingly boring place to be. Reassuring, almost.

What wasn't reassuring was Victoria Evans, the latest addition to the operation support team, a snoopy little woman who was already walking towards her holding a mug of coffee in each hand. "Hey, welcome back!"

Stephanie was sure she heard at least three exclamation marks. "Hey, Victoria, how're things?"

"I got you coffee!" Victoria presented her with one of the mugs, her face begging for approval. "White, one sugar, the way you like it."

Stephanie was a black-no-sugar kind of person through and through. She wasn't going to tell Victoria that, though. Instead, she took the mug with a smile and placed it on her desk. "That's very thoughtful," she said, already planning her quick escape to re-gift the coffee to the Ficus in the lobby.

"Well, you know, first day back and all, I thought you deserved a treat. I bet Scotland wasn't exactly a joyride," Victoria resumed, leaning on the desk with both hands, as if trying to push it down through the floor. She was clearly after something.

"You know I can't talk about it," replied Stephanie. There were strict rules about clearance levels, and Victoria's was as high as the basement.

"Oh, don't you go all corporate on me!" was the reply, accompanied by a wide grin. "I've seen the weather was a nightmare, and that's on the newscast, so hardly classified information!"

Her fake enthusiasm was starting to get on Stephanie's nerves. She forced herself to smile back. "Yes, we had quite a bit of rain." *No point in disappointing the audience*, she thought.

The comment seemed to be enough to make Victoria rather pleased with the interaction. She made to leave and Stephanie was about to turn on her laptop, when Victoria doubled back and leaned over the desk once again. "I almost forgot. The boss wants to see you."

That was neither specific nor informative. Also, she should have led with that. "The boss?"

"Mr Cook," she explained with some extra nodding. "The Chief of Operations. You know, our boss."

As if we were on the same level, thought Stephanie.

Victoria gave one last smile for the crowd, then was gone, out the door and to her desk in the next room.

Stephanie exhaled. Her hand automatically reached for the mug of coffee and took a sip, only to spit it back into the cup right away. "How do people even drink this?" she murmured to herself.

Leaving the pale brew on her desk, she stood up and marched to the Chief's office.

While field agents and operations staff shared an open floor office space, Edward Cook was the only one blessed with a door all for himself, the words *Chief of Operations* engraved on a shiny silver plaque, so as to prevent anyone forgetting who was in charge.

Cook wasn't at the top of the pyramid, yet Director and CEO Robert Millican was too busy playing golf to pay attention to what was happening at SafeOp Defence Services. Because his golf partners were the main source of business for the agency – and because his personality verged on the obnoxious type – it was a widespread feeling that he could be excused.

As for Stephanie, she didn't care much for Millican but was grateful for the Chief. He had welcomed her into the agency when she was little more than a teenager and mentored her through the years. It was thanks to him that she had become who she was.

After a couple of knocks, the Chief's voice invited her inside. She took care to close the door behind her.

"Davis, welcome back to base. I trust you've settled back in at your station already."

Stephanie thanked him politely, noticing how she wasn't being asked to sit. That was unusual, though she couldn't decide if it was a good or a bad sign. Either way, her interest was tickled.

"It's good to be back, sir. Evans even made me coffee," she offered. Victoria might have been new, but her coffee skills were already quite legendary.

The Chief furrowed his brows. "Oh dear, I'm sorry about that. What are you going to do about it?"

"The Ficus in the lobby looks a bit parched, sir," she replied.

He nodded, almost to himself. "Quite so, quite so." He stood up from his chair and walked around the desk, only to lean back against it, facing Stephanie. "What news from the Highlands?"

That all depended on what he meant by *news*. "No conclusive evidence of approach," she reported. "If an aircraft landed there, they must have taken off again before we got there."

"Could you at least confirm the beacon was activated?" he insisted.

She nodded. "We located the signal as originating near the Partridge Estate."

"I see." He dropped his head, deep in thought for a moment. "I will need you to leave today for your next assignment."

"Sir, there won't be time to complete the report for the last mission," she pointed out.

"You'll have to type fast," he replied. "An extra-terrestrial vehicle was discovered in the Forest of Dean on Sunday. Millican has taken an interest, and the site has been secured. There is an investigation going on. He asked for all resources set on the Highlands case to be redirected to the spacecraft in the Forest of Dean."

An *extra-terrestrial vehicle*. A *spacecraft*. Those words sounded odd in her head. Also, Sunday was three days after the signal from the Highlands' beacon had ceased. "Should I consider a connection to the Highlands, sir?"

She had been on two recon missions already to investigate suspicious sightings, both times hypothesising smugglers or terrorists. She had never considered something from another planet could be landing instead, and she certainly would have thought it a joke if it had been anybody else talking.

The Chief shook his head. "The beacon in the Highlands might have been a factor in directing them here. I wouldn't assume any further connection at this stage. As far as we know, the two events remain separate."

"Yes, sir."

He paused before adding, "Between you and I, Davis, I don't like how quickly Millican shut down the Highlands case as soon as he heard of it. Keep an open mind, would you?"

Stephanie nodded. "Was there anything piloting the vehicle?"

"Yes, there was a pilot," he said. "A small snake-like creature, if a snake had eight legs, that is. A treacherous little thing. Our science division is taking care of it."

He was choosing his words carefully. There was clearly only so much she was allowed to know. "Who found the vehicle?" she asked. He would tell her when she reached the boundaries of her clearance level.

"Three hikers. Two of them had physical contact with the vehicle, one of them with the pilot," he explained.

All sorts of alarm bells started ringing in Stephanie's mind. "What kind of physical contact? Was it an attack?"

The Chief sighed. "Would you call it an attack when the humans went knocking at the spaceship's door?"

Typical. Trust humans to play Earth ambassadors and poke at what they shouldn't. "Quarantine protocols?"

"Both of them are now held in a secure facility in the Mendips. They will remain there for four weeks, pending tests."

"The Mendips are quite a way away," she commented.

"It was either that or hold them in a room the size of a shoebox," he replied. "We thought we'd bring them somewhere with a garden space."

He sounded peeved, so Stephanie dropped the argument. "How are they coping?"

"They're not significantly worse than they were before meeting E.T."

With all due respect, that was lame. "Are we really naming

the case after an 80s film?"

The Chief glared at her. "The creature calls itself Skaara, or at least a member of a species called Skaara. One of the lab coats seems to have grown quite fond of it and goes around calling it Gwyn, go figure."

Suppose they had to call it something. "Should I understand the alien is of friendly nature?"

"On the contrary," he replied. "Anyone who comes in direct contact with the creature seems to lose focus and starts talking as if they were the wretched thing themselves."

"Are we talking psychosis?"

"More like mind control," he replied. "Although it seems to disappear as soon as the alien and the human are separated."

She chose to ignore her own scepticism at hearing the words *mind control*. "What about the hiker who found it? Was he harmed?"

"He's physically well, nothing more than a few scratches on his shoulders where the alien was holding on to him. No weird extra-planetary infections either, if you can believe it." He shook his head, as if he was the one who couldn't believe the humans' dumb luck. "Naturally, we're giving him psychiatric support to process the experience. The poor guy doesn't even remember the journey out of the woods."

Stephanie took a moment to process all that. "How are you sure he's not still under the alien's control?" she asked. She was picturing a zombie-like young man walking the halls of the base, pretending to act human while an alien parasite leeched on his brain.

"The alien is securely locked away, and the hikers have been separated and confined to their quarters. We've done tests. The creature's sway only works if it's touching the person," he reiterated. "We've taken precautions, Davis."

Stephanie straightened up and held her tongue against further questions.

In the short silence that followed, she took a moment to gather her thoughts. A spaceship sighting didn't have to be a threat. An extra-terrestrial creature landing on Earth still didn't have to be a threat. Even telepathy could just be seen as a fun game. Mind control, however, was something else.

The Chief exhaled, his shoulder sagging for a moment under the weight of it all. "The laboratory and the quarantined quarters have been set up at the same base. I know what you're thinking, and I'm not excited about it either, but Millican has taken charge, and he thinks it's a brilliant idea. The science team is running tests on all subjects."

Stephanie nodded, yet her mind was still elaborating on the information. "It can control you only if it touches you."

"Quite so."

"Then it's likely it can't control more than one person at a time."

"We're still investigating that," he replied.

That cautionary tone again. Stephanie had to tread lightly. "What are my orders, Chief?" she asked, placing him back on the pedestal and rebalancing the equation.

He straightened up and crossed his arms. "Take base in the Mendips and question the subjects. The alien didn't kill them, so it's possible there's something else it wants. Find out what that is and report to me directly. Understood?"

Stephanie nodded. "Understood, sir."

* * *

The subjects quarantined at the Mendip base were Frank and Lucy Campbell, siblings who had stumbled on the alien space-craft on a Sunday hike and had taken it upon themselves to welcome the visitors to rainy old England.

He was a highly-praised PhD student of Chemistry at the University of Bristol. She never graduated secondary school, had a criminal record, and her residential address was a friend's couch.

The call to SafeOp Defence Services had been made by the third hiker, Matthew Cavell, supposedly Miss Campbell's boyfriend.

According to the first response team, Mr Cavell hadn't followed his sweetheart into the clearing, leaving the siblings to explore the findings on their own. Once at the base, in reward to either his wealth or his smarts, he hadn't faced more than half an hour in a doctor's office before signing a non-disclosure agreement and riding off in his father's Mercedes.

As influential as Mr Cavell could be, it was odd how easily his son had gotten out of the whole business – unless Millican had been involved. Not to mention, there was something familiar about the name. Anthony Cavell, father of Matthew Cavell and married to Lady Eliza Jane Cavell. He couldn't have been a nobody. The call had been made directly to SafeOp, so maybe one of Millican's connections.

A full search of the agency database was going to give her some answers. She put a pin on it for the time being.

The first person she was going to talk to was Frank Campbell. He had been confined to his quarters: a couple of rooms and a small yard where he could stretch his legs and get some fresh air.

The room chosen for the interrogation had been partitioned

by a plastic wall, which separated Stephanie's allocated side from Frank's. A couple of measured openings were strategically placed to allow them to talk to each other. It wasn't the warmest room, neither by temperature nor by atmosphere. She made a mental note to ask for an upgrade – there was no point in treating these people like criminals.

She sat down at the table and opened the thin folder containing all that Frank had remembered of the events. It wasn't much. The psych evaluation was longer than the witness statement.

When the door opened on the other side of the plastic partition, a tall young man hesitated on the threshold.

Stephanie stood up to welcome him. "Frank, please come in. I'm Agent Davis of SafeOp Defence Services. How are you?"

He nodded, pressing his lips together in an uncertain smile. "Yeah, fine. Thanks." He closed the door on the escort agent standing behind him and sat down at the table.

"Normally I'd get you coffee, but I wasn't sure you would want that," she added with half a smile, returning to her seat.

"Is that even allowed? I'm a potential biohazard," he replied, his tone full of resignation. His arms were stretched on the table, right thumb forcefully rubbing into the palm of his left hand. "It's okay, anyway. I already had one."

Stephanie cleared her throat and leaned forward on the table. "Before we start, there's some formalities we need to go through," she said. "There are cameras recording in this room, and this conversation will be recorded and used as part of the investigation into the extra-terrestrial landing in the Forest of Dean."

Frank blinked at her, unresponsive.

"Do you consent?"

23

"Yes, of course," he replied. His thumb was rubbing the palm of his hand. "Listen, I don't know what happened. That thing took hold of me, and it just went dark."

"I know," intervened Stephanie. "Your statement is very clear about that, and it's okay."

He wasn't listening. "I wish I could tell you more, but I really don't know what happened," he repeated, as if to himself.

It was hard to understand across the plastic partition, but Stephanie could see that he was stuck in a loop. She had to take him out of the small burrow of guilt he had made for himself if she wanted to get anything out of him. "What is the last thing you remember?"

"Looking into the opening, I guess," he offered. "I couldn't see anything, but I remember thinking there was something hiding in the dark. Never thought I'd regret being right."

"Do you remember seeing the Skaara?"

He exhaled and shook his head. "It's weird," he said, then paused, lips parted as if words were due out any second.

"What is weird?" she encouraged him.

"I don't remember seeing the, you know, the alien," he continued, "but I know what it's like. Not as in what it looks like, but what it feels like." He shook his head. "It sounds crazy, doesn't it?"

"We're talking about an extra-terrestrial creature landing on Earth and mind-controlling people. I think we passed the line of crazy a while back," she said with a smile, trying to encourage him.

Frank looked unconvinced. His eyes roamed the room, as if trying to get a grip on thin air, just like his mind was likely trying to get a hold of memories that weren't memories after all. "The thing is, I don't *remember* any of it. It's like I dreamt

24

about it and then I woke up, and the dream kind of stayed with me, but I couldn't say what it was that I was dreaming of. Do you know what I mean?"

Stephanie leaned forward on the table. "I think so."

He bit his lips and furrowed his brow, then continued, "If the thing took hold of my brain, it's possible it left some kind of impression. An after-image, maybe."

"Let me see if I get it. You mean like when you walk on fresh snow and leave your footprints behind. You can't remember the creature, but you can still see the footprints."

He nodded.

Stephanie glanced down at the file, which was open in front of her. None of what Frank was telling her had made it into the notes. "What is the next thing you remember, after the creature got hold of you?"

"Waking up in my room, here in this place," he replied. "As I said, I don't remember anything that happened in between."

"No, I know," interrupted Stephanie. He was getting frustrated once again, with his arms wrapped around his chest, defending himself against the humiliation of not having all the answers. She softened her tone and said, "Your sister remembers well enough, so it's not a problem that you don't."

He looked up, surprised. "My sister told you what happened?"

Stephanie ignored his reaction and carried on. "Also, that's not what I'm after."

A confused frown wrinkled Frank's forehead.

"Your friend Matthew is the one who organised the hike for the three of you, isn't he?"

"What are you getting at? That we went alien-hunting in the forest or something?"

Stephanie could see him stiffening through the plastic barrier. "I'm just trying to put the pieces together. Do you know why he chose that particular trail?"

The way Frank breathed out of his nose reminded Stephanie of an enraged bull. "Is that all you care about?" he snapped. "Placing the blame on somebody? It was his mother who came up with the idea. Matthew has done nothing wrong. Leave him alone."

Interesting, thought Stephanie. The psych evaluation mentioned something about the young man's attachment to his sister's boyfriend, but this hit a whole new level.

"Let's talk about something else," she said with a wave of her hand. "You compared the experience to waking up from a dream."

"I was never asleep," he replied drily.

"How would you rather describe it?"

He hesitated, pursed his lips, then shook his head. "I don't know. I remember feeling helpless. Something was pulling me down, or backwards, I mean, away from the real world. I couldn't figure out where I was. I couldn't see anything. I couldn't feel anything around me. It was all dark, and empty. And silent."

He didn't look enraged anymore, but the more he talked, the more his frustration grew. When his voice started to crack, he stopped talking. His hands went to rest on his lap, where he rubbed his palms for a moment, before catching himself and bringing them under his thighs, locked against the seat of the chair.

It was hard to see clearly through the plastic wall, but Stephanie thought Frank's eyes looked shinier than they had before, as if he was on the verge of tears. The Skaara hadn't just been guiding his actions; it had held back his whole persona, closed him in a box, deprived him of all senses, for hours.

"How do you think the creature did that?" she asked. "I mean, from a biochemical perspective. You're a scientist. You must have thought about it. What do you think brought you to such a complete sensory deprivation?"

She didn't need the answer – the science team had already theorised a whole encyclopaedia about it – but it was worth a shot, if it brought Frank out of the downward spiral he was sliding on.

Slowly, he leaned forward and rested his elbows on the table. "Well, I'm not a neuroscientist, but I know there are areas of the brain that are responsible for our relationship with the environment. If the..." He paused, took a breath, then continued, "If the Skaara took hold of the central nervous system, controlling the voluntary impulses and leaving the autonomous system to keep life support functions online, I suspect that might explain the sensory deprivation and, you know, everything else."

Stephanie nodded. "A bit like being kidnapped and thrown in the boot of your own car."

"Except I couldn't even feel the turns and bumps in the road," he corrected.

"It sounds terrifying." Truth was, she knew that feeling way too well, back when she still trusted people, until the one she trusted most turned his gun on her and locked her in the boot of the car.

Frank's boot might have been metaphorical, but she doubted it had been any less scarring.

Both sat back in silence for a few moments. The room was still carrying the words, and Stephanie was gathering them, placing each piece in its spot, trying to push the memory of the boot out of her mind.

"The thing is," started Frank, then hesitated as he looked for the right words. "The thing is, I don't think it wants to harm anyone."

Stephanie didn't think so either. "Could you elaborate on that?"

Frank, however, shook his head, like he couldn't see a way to do that. He started saying something a couple of times, then changed his mind. Finally, he said, "You know that feeling when somebody walks into your room when you're not there?"

If there was a connection, Stephanie wasn't seeing it yet. "Go on," she encouraged.

"You walk into your room, and everything looks the same, and nothing has been touched, but there's something in the air that tells you somebody has been there, that the space is not as safe as you thought it was."

For being a science guy, he's good with metaphors, thought Stephanie. "How can you be sure everything is the same?" she asked, trying to follow the thread. "Maybe the intruder stole one of your socks, and you won't ever find out."

There was a pause. Frank was giving it some thought. In a metaphor where memories were socks, he was likely counting how many he had left in his drawer.

"Do you think the alien was rummaging around your sock drawer?" she asked.

For a moment, it looked as if Frank hadn't heard the question. Then he said, "It felt like that when I woke up. As if someone had invaded my personal space." He scoffed. "Heck, it was in my *head*. It wasn't just my personal space that thing invaded."

As she noticed Frank's hands clenching into fists, Stephanie

28

decided it was a good moment to drop the topic. "We're going to stop here for today," she said. "With your permission, I'd like to pass the recording of this conversation to your assigned psychologist."

"Yeah, sure."

There wasn't much more Stephanie could get from him, so she was about to stand up when he asked, "What happened to Matt?"

She settled back down, elbows on the table. "He gave his statement and went home."

He seemed pacified by the answer. Odd that he didn't already know.

"And my sister?" he persisted.

"Quarantined, just like you are."

"Is she okay?"

All tests came out clear, if that was what he meant. "She's okay."

There wasn't much more to say, and Frank understood that. He let the escort bring him back to his quarters without as much as a wave back to her.

* * *

Later that day, sitting at her desk, writing her report of the interrogation, Stephanie couldn't stop thinking about the metaphor of the intruder in the room.

She doubted the Skaara's plan was for world domination, and yet a crew of one only made sense as a scout mission, a single spaceship sent to gather intel before a larger fleet came flying

FIRST ALIEN

across the sky.

If that was the case, there was no way of knowing what kind of information the alien could have found in Frank's mind. Even so, it all depended on what the Skaara were after. Considering how easily it had taken control of the human brain on the first try, massacre didn't have to be an option. Mass enslavement, however, seemed very likely.

It was already dark outside when she wrote the last line of the report and turned off her laptop. Everyone had already left the base, with the exception of the security guards and the quarantined siblings.

The Skaara was under lock and key on the east corridor of the ground floor. Stephanie had read all about it, yet she still hadn't had a chance to see the creeper from outer space with her own eyes.

She walked to the reinforced double door at the end of the hall and used her pass to open it. There wasn't any specific reason for her to be there, except the need for a reality check, to clear all doubts that the alien really existed. It wasn't a figment of anybody's imagination, nor an elaborate prank of some sort.

When she walked into the laboratory, the creature was huddled in the corner of three concentrical boxes. It looked to be fast asleep, its long, thin body coiled up on itself. Not one of the spare hairs on the creature's back was moving. It must have been hiding its legs between the coils because, from where she was standing, it looked no different than a snake, albeit an ugly one.

Even though she couldn't see its eyes, Stephanie was sure she had the Skaara's full attention.

Even if a bit on the small side, Lucy's lodgings at the base were almost comfortable. After weeks of precarious lodging in someone's living room, at least she was sleeping on a real bed and had her own bathroom. It was practically luxury.

As for entertainment, someone with a wicked sense of humour thought she could spend her time gardening. The only thing she knew about plants was that they were green, mostly.

It took some convincing to get a TV and a small supply of books. Even then, the TV was straight out of the 1980s, and the books were all sappy historical fiction novels. For pastime, she had started drawing obscene pictures on the margins, the pleasure only partially fading when she realised nobody was ever going to awkwardly enjoy her art. *A shame, really*, she thought.

When they had thrown her in there, her escort had taken everything away from her, including her clothes. All needed testing, they had said. Lucy failed to see how testing her socks was going to bring any enlightenment on the alien menace. She had been left wearing SafeOp spare uniforms and underwear, which would have been fine, if they hadn't been dramatically oversized.

Her mobile and gadgets were also gone as soon as she walked

through the door. She wasn't even given the chance to message anybody to make sure they knew she hadn't been abducted by aliens – not yet, at least.

A week after she arrived, cabin fever started creeping in. More and more often, Lucy lay awake on the lumpy bed, her sleep haunted by the memory of Frank's absent stare while the alien spoke through his mouth.

She spent her time waiting for someone to knock on her door and lead her either to the next questioning or to her assigned therapist. She wasn't going to talk to anybody, but at least it took her mind off her nightmares, so she hadn't protested too much.

The small outdoor space she had been allowed – the very one they had called a garden – was a small patch of green, surrounded by a mesh fence twice her height. Apart from the dirty drawings, sitting on the grass was the only thing keeping her sane.

Because of the pain she had suffered during the hike in the woods, her back was still giving her grief. She had thought about asking for a yoga mat, then she remembered she wasn't a yoga kind of person. A massage was something she would've enjoyed, but the service wasn't in the catalogue.

What worried Lucy the most was the fact that she hadn't seen her brother since they had been brought there, let alone talked to him. She had protested with all her might – they were there for the same reason, after all – but she had met with a concrete wall. Apparently, being possessed by an alien snake was enough to earn a next-level sort of isolation.

On top of that, it wasn't the government that was running the operation. Someone had those SafeOp over-weaponised bouncers on their payroll. Lucy would've given her pinkie toe to know who was pulling the strings and why they were doing that.

That was where the paranoia came in. There were secret labs and secret experiments, and it was too easy to believe that the quarantine gig was a convenient excuse to keep them there and use them as guinea pigs to study the alien, then dispose of them once they were done. If anyone asked, the extra-terrestrial creeper could very well get the blame for their disappearance.

It took days of harmless testing and no sign of experimentation before Lucy figured that line of overthinking was probably going too far.

As for Matthew, he had disappeared as soon as his father's fancy car had shown up. After that, the lack of a mobile had seriously affected their communication. She told herself she was too mad at him to care, yet she still wished she could call him to tell him that.

A knock on the door interrupted her train of thought. She was lying on the bed and barely glanced over to ask, "Who's there?"

Her eyes lingered on the ceiling, where a darker patch of paint made her think of a rabbit riding a motorcycle.

The door clicked open. She slowly sat up on the bed, twisting her back from side to side in a futile attempt at easing the pain. A security agent was standing to attention by the doorway, his face covered by a protective visor while a suit covered the rest of his body. It was the kind of PPE Gucci would've designed.

"You know," she said, "it's good manners to wait to be invited in before opening the door to a lady's room. What if I was naked?"

"You aren't."

She scoffed. "You could at least have brought me pizza. Any

33

news from the canteen? Please give me hope."

From that distance, she couldn't see if the agent's expression had changed behind the visor. She liked to think it had.

"You can request to see our medic, you know?" he said. He must have noticed her wincing in pain.

"And fill my stomach with painkillers. Yes, that sounds lovely," she replied drily. She wasn't going to give them any excuse to drug her senseless.

He shook his head. "You're wanted in the interrogation room."

Lucy exhaled. "Who is it this time? Squirrel Face, or Moustache Man? No, don't tell me. I live for the surprise."

"Randall and Lee have left the base. You're going to make a new friend, missy."

Lucy stood up and glared all the way to the agent. When she got close enough for her nose to touch the plastic visor, she whispered, "Call me *missy* one more time, and I'll turn your nose inside out."

Through the screen, she was sure she saw a hint of a frown as he tried to process how that would work.

"How about you don't threaten me, and I don't restrain you?" he replied.

"What, are you scared this little girl might hurt you?"

She heard the agent sigh before he grabbed her arm, and her whole body turned around, her arm twisted behind her back. Handcuffs snapped on her wrists before she could even think about reacting.

"Seriously? I thought we were friends, Glass Head!"

"It's not glass," he remarked. "Now move along."

He led her down the empty grey hall. It was an ugly stretch of corridor to the only other room she was allowed in, since the rest of the base excluded potentially contaminated humans. The neon lights didn't add any interesting brush to the depressing tinge. When they arrived at the door, the agent let Lucy in the interrogation room and took off the handcuffs.

She had thought up one last joke to throw at him, but the door was already closing by the time she opened her mouth..

"I guess I'll have fun on my own," she murmured to the empty room, absent-mindedly massaging her wrists.

The quarantined half of the room was separated from the rest of the world by a plastic wall, as usual. She went to stand closer, then breathed against it. Her breath condensed on the surface. She watched it slowly fade, then pressed her palm against the plastic and pushed, wondering what it would take to break it down.

She turned around to check the room. There had been some improvements since the last time she had been there. The table was still there, pressed against the transparent plastic barrier to give the illusion of continuity with the one on the other side. Another constant was the chair, which was in the run for most uncomfortable chair in the country.

The exciting new addition was in the form of a money tree stuck in a vase in the corner of the room, like a cheap attempt at showing how caring they could be because they managed to keep a plant alive. She walked up to it. It was almost as tall as she was.

When the door opened on the other side, Lucy turned around to see a woman walking in, looking slim in her dark blazer. She was carrying a few thin folders of paperwork in one hand and a mug of coffee in the other.

Almost at the same time, the door on her side of the wall opened, and Not-Glass-Head walked in with a mug of coffee, which he left on the table for her before leaving again.

Lucy stood frozen for a moment. She wasn't sure what had just happened. Nobody had ever arranged for coffees in the interrogation room. She didn't even think that was allowed.

"I'm Agent Stephanie Davis of SafeOp Defence Services. I was hoping we could have a chat about what happened to your brother," the woman said, then gestured for Lucy to take a seat.

It was never just a chat, not really. Especially when they had bothered bringing in someone new. Lucy walked around the table and went to stand against the plastic wall. She had to make a point. If they thought she was just going to do what she was told, they had another thing coming.

Davis seemed to hesitate, then nodded and walked up to the wall as well. For a few seconds, it was just short of a staring contest.

"Before we begin," started Davis, but Lucy already knew the line.

"Don't tell me, there are cameras in here, and you're recording every word. What else is new?" Her tone flat, she kept her gaze on the woman, almost challenging her to continue.

A muscle flexed as Davis clenched her jaw. "Do you consent to that?"

"Do I have a choice? What happens if I don't, Blazer Lady?"

Davis raised her eyebrows at the nickname, then lowered her gaze and sighed. Lucy couldn't suppress a smirk. An easy win for her.

Eyes still fixed on the file open on the table, the agent said, "I guess we could tighten your quarantine and lock you in your room until further notice. Considering the circumstances, it would be easy to keep you here under charges of obstruction of justice, with potential threat to the nation, if not the entire planet."

The air froze around Lucy. She couldn't have heard right. "You can't do that."

"I wouldn't be too sure."

The room was getting smaller around her. "You're not the police. You have no authority to do that."

Only then did Davis look at her. "Authority, you say? An extra-terrestrial spacecraft landed on Earth, and the only person who had a chance to communicate with the pilot is the same person who is refusing to talk." She paused for effect, bringing her face up close to the plastic wall between them. "It seems to me like you're colluding with the alien invader."

"Bullshit!" burst Lucy, recoiling in the impetus. "She's not even invading. You cannot just make things up like that. I want my lawyer."

A lawyer. What a stupid thing to say. As if she had a right to a lawyer in England's very own Area 51.

Davis didn't even flinch. "What do you mean she's not invading?"

Lucy's hands closed in tight fists. "I didn't consent."

The agent held her gaze. She probably thought of herself as a badass.

In spite of herself, Lucy couldn't hold eye contact. Far from throwing in the towel, she said with a snarl, "Fine, I'm okay with Big Brother watching me."

She wasn't scared. She was doing Davis a favour. Yet, she could almost sense the agent gloating behind her serious snout. "I spoke with your brother yesterday."

"He's still alive, then," commented Lucy, hiding her worries behind sarcasm.

Davis ignored that. She picked up and opened another

one of the files she was carrying and continued, "He doesn't remember anything of the events, but you were with him the whole time. And you spoke with him."

"Is that a question?"

Davis looked up briefly. "No."

Good, because Lucy didn't want to talk about it. It was enough to relive the scene anytime she closed her eyes – the alien shooting out of the opening, her brother held in standby, his eyes going glassy, and the creeper talking through him. Sometimes, in her worst nightmares, the alien left her brother to jump onto her.

She knew the creeper had been put into a cage – she had been told that much – yet that wasn't at all reassuring. She wondered how long it would be before they threw it at Frank again, if they weren't doing that already on a regular basis. She'd never know if that happened. She'd be sitting in a room just like that one, powering through annoying questions she didn't want to answer, and with nothing new to tell them.

The whole story was in the statement she had given when she had been brought in. Every aspect and every word, which was a first in her experience of interrogations. It hadn't been enough, though, and everyone was still accusing her of withholding information. Fucking typical. Davis was probably trying to be smart, looking for a way to make her talk, as if the core of her training had been watching re-runs of Detective Poirot.

It was all a ruse anyway. They were always going to lock her up, her brother too. Even once they were done with their testing, there was no getting out of there.

Davis took a sip of her coffee, then nodded at Lucy's. "Aren't you going to drink?"

"I don't like coffee," lied Lucy.

"Now, that's bullshit."

A simple statement, as if teaching her what bullshit looked like. Lucy caught herself flinching at the language. Blazer Lady knew swear words.

"You drink coffee like your life depends on it," Davis continued. "You even asked for coffee during the last interrogation, when they called you in earlier than usual and you had to wait five whole minutes for Randall to show up." She paused, a smug look on her face. "As you can see, I've done my homework."

That was an unexpected comeback. Lucy struggled to hide her surprise. "Am I supposed to be impressed?" she managed.

"Oh, but you are."

She looked proud of what she had just accomplished, and Lucy resented her for it. That was usually her kind of game. This smartass was using her tricks.

Lucy turned to her side and leaned back against the table, crossing her arms. "I have nothing to say that I haven't already said," she stated.

She expected Davis to press on, or try another of her insightful remarks, but that didn't happen. Instead, she asked, "You and your brother were on that hike with your boyfriend, Matthew Cavell. Was it him who suggested the hike?"

No, Lucy wasn't going to fall for that. She might have been mad at Matt for leaving her there without a word, but she wasn't going to drop him in it.

It was a long minute of stubborn silence before Davis finally exhaled and closed the file. "You're looking at this the wrong way, Campbell. Nobody's out here to get you. I'll let you think about it. I'll be back when you're ready to talk."

She walked to the door and left.

Lucy exhaled in the empty room. She hadn't realised how

much tension she had built up, and now her shoulders felt stiff, her neck was a bundle of nerves, and her overall frame was shaking in frustration. She glanced at the coffee mug on the table. She knew it hadn't been spiked or anything – they fed her every day, after all. It was nothing worst than yet another attempt at gaining her trust. As if she'd melt and fall to Blazer Lady's feet only because she had been brought coffee.

Still, Davis was right. Lucy lived for coffee. She took a sip and focused on disliking the warm brew. Annoyingly, it was just as she liked it – black and sweet, but only one and a half sugars, because she was not a psycho.

She sat at the table sipping her coffee, waiting for someone to pick her up and take her back.

When the door opened again on the other side of the plastic barrier, a man walked in, tall and egg-shaped, sporting the hair of a twelve-year-old – which was either impressive, or fake.

"Agent Davis, you've changed," she mocked him, her straight face aimed at telling him how unimpressed she was by that turn of events. If that was Davis' sidekick, she wasn't going to give him an easier time.

"I am not Agent Davis," he replied stiffly.

"Yes, I can see that," she replied. Her eyes narrowed to a slit. It was hard to understand if the new guy was being serious. After a moment of silence, she thought she should clarify. "It was a joke."

To her surprise, the man gave a stunted chuckle. "I see. That's a good joke."

No, it wasn't. She took another sip of her coffee, then stood up to face the new opponent. Something was not right about him, and not just his sense of humour.

"I'm Edward Cook," he said. "I'm in charge of this operation.

Agent Davis won't be coming back in here, if that's what you were expecting."

"I wasn't," she lied. "She gave up that easily, did she?"

Edward Cook's eyes widened, then narrowed in thought. "Davis doesn't give up. Once she sets her mind on a target, she's trained to achieve it."

Lucy frowned. It was a strange way of delivering that line, but it checked out with Lucy's first impression – not so much with the turn of events. "Why is it you're here instead, then?"

"Davis has to follow orders. I pulled rank, you might say."

She kept sipping her coffee, trying to show how little she cared. "Should I be flattered?"

When she looked at him again, the man's lips were smiling. It was the only part of his face that was doing that. His eyes were barely alive. She had seen that look before, on Frank's face. For once, she was grateful for the plastic barrier between them.

She placed the mug back on the table. "Why do I get the feeling we have met before?"

He was unfazed. "I meet a lot of people."

She cocked her head to the side. "I bet you do."

Cook's smile disappeared, replaced by an equally disturbing frown. He could have been planning her murder or trying to figure out some third-degree equation. Finally, he nodded and reinstated the stilted grin. "I need you to do something for me."

"No shit."

The man shook his head. "No, it doesn't involve excrements."

Lucy had to suppress a laugh. She hadn't expected that. "Good," she managed. Then something else came to her mind.

"Let me see my brother, and I'll help you."

"I thought you'd ask for that."

"Yes, because nobody has let me see him yet."

He didn't reply.

Lucy endured that moment of silence, knowing full well she couldn't be the first to break it. Her gaze was fixed on Cook's empty eyes, piercing a hole in the plastic barrier.

Then he relaxed, exhaled, and leaned forward. "I'm sorry about that. Quarantine is as annoying for you as it is for me. However, there seems to be all sorts of reasons why you and your brother can't be in the same room."

All sorts of reasons sounded like all sorts of nonsense. "Yeah, I bet it's annoying for you. Really thwarting the Skaara's plans to take over the place and conquer the world."

"The Skaara don't conquer."

"No, they holiday. I'm sure that'll make the military love these creepers and welcome them as their saviours."

"You believe that to be true?" he asked, raising his eyebrows.

"What? No!" Lucy gave a sigh. "Jeez, you really have to learn sarcasm."

Cook hesitated. She could almost hear his infected brain cells trying to work through the concept. Eventually he nodded. "Sarcasm means you said the opposite of what you believe."

"Yes, genius. That is correct."

"It sounds like lying."

Something in the man's face looked like disappointment. Lucy started wondering why the little alien had put so much effort into reaching out to her.

"What do you want from me?" she asked, then braced herself as the smile reappeared on Cook's face.

He reached into his jacket's breast pocket. Lucy heard a click as he took a pen out, then placed it on the table. Odd how she hadn't noticed the buzzing sound until it was gone. She glanced up at the security cameras. If any of them were functioning, she couldn't tell.

Cook took a seat at the table and gestured for her to do the same. "We need to return to the vessel."

She sat down opposite him, then took another sip of coffee. "By *vessel* you mean spaceship?" she taunted him. "Why don't you just order somebody to take you there? You're in charge of operations, remember? You can make people do things."

"Yet there are people this human has to report to as well," he replied, his voice flat and slow, a bored mannequin talking to himself. "When I gave that order, I was met with a warning. Another attempt and somebody else would be put in charge, this body no longer allowed on the premises."

"Have you thought about going there yourself? You figured out how to talk; you can figure out how to drive a car, I'm sure."

"My main body is still in the laboratory."

Lucy was on her feet before she knew it, barely noticing the clang of the chair falling backwards. She held up her hands as if the plastic barrier wasn't enough on its own. "Hold up. You mean your fancy puppet here is in remote control? What the actual fuck?"

"No need to be alarmed. I will show you," the alien said. Cook stood up, carefully moving his chair out of the way, then turned around and lifted a wisp of hair, exposing the nape of his neck. A dark nugget was nested deep in the skin. "It's only a small appendix. An extra brain, so to speak."

It was a part of the alien. That thing planted in Cook's neck was part of an alien. She couldn't see his face, but she was sure he was sniggering – an alien sniggering. Surely the science

43

guys must have noticed. Lucy imagined an amputated alien creeper sitting quietly in its cage while scientists frantically tried to locate whichever bit of its body had fallen off. The idea was both ridiculous and terrifying at the same time.

"How does it work?" she asked.

"You don't need to know," he said, turning back to face her.

"Well, that sucks, because I really do want to know," she replied, taking an aggressive step forward. She had to know if she was scheduled to get an extra brain of her own. "You see, I could be your ticket out of here, but I don't appreciate alien overlords driving me around like I'm some kind of Japanese robot."

"Should I believe that you would stand against your own kind, of your own free will?"

It sounded way worse when Cook said it out loud. "I stand on my own side, like I always have," she replied. "Now, are you going to tell me what's the magic trick there?"

"It's a satellite brain," he said slowly.

"Yeah, you said that. Do you have, like, a whole arsenal of those?"

"There is a single appendix I can use for this purpose."

Well, that was a small mercy. "And can you, like, from wherever your actual body is, can you see what's happening here?" she pressed on. "Like, I don't know, telepathy or something."

"It's a possibility."

It was like pulling a tooth out; each question was met with a slow and methodical answer. She clenched her fists. "Are you doing it now?"

"Am I doing what now?"

The desire to punch the answers out of him was becoming

overwhelming. "The telepathy thing. Are you seeing through his eyes and feeding him lines?" She hesitated at the next thought that came to her mind. "Are you doing to him what you did to my brother?"

The moment stretched. "Yes."

A chill ran down Lucy's spine. If that thing had a remote-control function, she was already screwed. "Let's say I agree to do this thing for you. What makes you think I can pull this off?"

"You're a thief. It's in your file," he replied.

Of course, she thought. She got arrested once for stealing her own mother's necklace, and suddenly she was the reincarnation of Diabolik. "I'm not that kind of thief."

The frown on Cook's face looked genuine. "You steal things. I need you to steal something. Are you not the kind of thief that steals things?"

"Let me rephrase that," she started, taking another step closer to the plastic wall between them. "How do you think I'm going to get out of my quarters, which are locked, then into the laboratory, which is locked, out of the cage that – guess what? – is locked, and then out of the whole freaking compound, which is not only locked, but heavily guarded with people who would love to either shoot me or arrest me?"

He waved the whole thing off. "That won't be a problem."

"It won't be *your* problem. I can see that."

"I'll make arrangements."

Almost reassuring, she thought. She needed more than that, though. "If anything goes wrong," she carried on, "I'm done for life, however short that life might be. I'm going to need some incentive."

Cook gave a pensive nod. "I see." He paused, his hands going to his pockets in a surprisingly human gesture. "I can guarantee the termination of your quarantine with something that is not your death."

Such drama. Lucy had to make an effort not to roll her eyes. "That was kind of a given. I can't take you out if I'm dead, can I? The thing is you don't really have a better option. You wouldn't be asking me if you did. I am your only shot, because I'm willing to do this without a creepy radio nugget buried in my brain, and because I haven't gotten myself a warning for screwing it up the first time."

"You are not the only option, just the most convenient," he remarked. "And it's not radio."

Lucy scoffed. "Yeah, right, and why am I the most convenient? I bet you couldn't hold control over another person if you tried, and that is a massive flaw in your masterplan, isn't it?"

She paused and took a breath. The man behind the plastic wall wasn't moving, so Lucy pressed on. "I come at a cost, and you're going to have to pay for it, whether you like it or not."

"You are not my only chance. Only the most convenient. And if money is the cost you mention, I can arrange for that."

Lucy crossed her arms. Money wasn't the matter. Still, if he was willing, it couldn't hurt. "Fifty thousand, and you clear my criminal record."

He gave it a few moments' thought. "Agreed."

Next, the big ask. "I want to see my brother. I'll do what you ask if you let me see my brother first."

"No."

"What? Why?"

"That would give you a chance to tell him what we're planning."

46

Yes, that's the whole point, genius. Lucy set her jaw and managed to keep a straight face. She decided the rules of the game. "Then I'll tell everything to the escort that'll take me back to my room. This way, we won't have that problem with Frankie."

Lucy could hear her own heart beating somewhere inside her ear. Behind the plastic barrier, Cook's body looked like a mannequin in a shop window, his eyes glazed over.

Eventually, he said, "I will arrange for a meeting. Your conversation will be monitored. If you say anything that might hint to this conversation, your quarantine will be extended and tightened."

So long as I get to see him, she thought.

"Your concern for him is unnecessary," he continued. "Your brother wasn't harmed. Once I lost physical contact, he was himself again."

"Well, I don't know," replied Lucy. "You're stuck in a lab and still puppeteering the big guy over here."

"I already explained there's only one satellite brain I can use for this purpose. Isn't that reassuring enough for you?"

"Are you expecting me to trust your word?"

Cook exhaled. "Your brother has been subject to all the physical and neurological tests you have and more. If there was a part of me anywhere about his body, it would have been found by now, wouldn't you agree?"

Patronising tone aside, it made sense. "Fine," she conceded. "There's only one tiny issue left."

Cook's jaw clenched visibly. Lucy ignored that.

"I'm not allowed out of my room without an escort. How am I getting you out of here?"

"One week from today, you'll be dismissed. Everything will

47

be in place by then."

Seven days to bye-bye. Just in time for the Christmas market, how considerate. "It would make sense to release my brother at the same time too, wouldn't you agree?" she tried, echoing his tone from earlier. "It would look suspicious if I was the only one leaving."

A pause. Cook's eyes went glassy while the alien calculated the odds. It was a terrifying sight. "That can be arranged," he finally confirmed.

Lucy found herself smiling. "Sounds like we have a deal."

He adjusted his jacket. "It appears we do."

He picked up the pen from the table and settled it back in the inside pocket of his jacket. Lucy thought she heard a click, although it could have been her imagination. She looked up to see the red light of the cameras turn back on. A soft static buzz filled the air.

Silently, he walked over to the door. "I'll have you escorted back to your room," he said as he opened it to leave.

When the door closed on the empty side of the room, Lucy felt her knees buckle. She leaned against the table, then went to sit on the chair. She didn't know how she had managed that, but she was sure she had stretched her luck as far as she could.

The mug of coffee was lying tepid in front of her. Maybe it would have been wiser to give Davis a chance instead of bargaining with the Skaara. On the other hand, it probably wouldn't have mattered anyway, when Cook only had to swoop in and pull rank like he had.

She sat back on the chair, and a sharp pain shot up her spine. The cherry on top of that whole mess.

Worst. Chair. Ever.

- IV -

It had taken Stephanie the rest of the day and a whole night to get over her frustration. Sitting in her appointed office at the base, she looked out the window. The autumn colours shone bright in the morning dew.

The Chief should have left her to do her job instead of taking Lucy's interrogation away from her. He had called it standard procedure, under the circumstances. That was not how standard procedure worked, Stephanie was sure.

It didn't matter anyway, she decided. The Chief must have had good reasons, even if they seemed to defy logic at the moment. Better do what he said.

At least she was still in charge of Frank's questioning. Even if he didn't remember the events, Stephanie was sure there was a lot he could tell her – maybe enough to understand what had brought the Skaara to Earth, or maybe some hints as to how to counteract the alien's mind-control.

The third hiker was another dark corner Frank might have been able to shed light on. Stephanie had requested the file on Matthew Cavell, something that appeared surprisingly difficult to obtain. Even in the reports about the finding of the spacecraft, he was no more than a side note, yet she was sure there was more to him than just a love for walks in the woods.

With a couple of hours to spare before her catch-up with the science team, Stephanie opened the transcript file of the conversation between Lucy and the Chief. It wasn't a long document, but it was at least something.

She glanced at it, already knowing what the page would tell her. The Chief had tried to get Lucy to cooperate, and she had demanded to see her brother. Predictable.

She checked the duration of the interview. The Chief had entered the room at 11:41 and left at 11:57, making it look as if most of those sixteen minutes had been spent in obstinate silence. She wouldn't have put it past Lucy, but Edward Cook wasn't the kind to sit patiently for that long.

With the document was a video file. She opened it and put on her earphones. The video started with Lucy sitting at the table, sipping her coffee. The camera was on the opposite corner of the room, so her figure looked slightly distorted by the plastic barrier.

A moment later, the Chief made his appearance. A brief exchange, then Lucy stood up. She asked to see her brother. He said no. Lucy went for a sarcastic comment, and the Chief seemed to take it seriously – that was odd.

Four minutes into the video, the Chief reached for something in his jacket. As he did so, the image flickered, and the video skipped ahead. All looked the same, yet twelve whole minutes had just gone unaccounted for, and the interview was about to end.

Stephanie brought the video back a few seconds and, sure enough, the seek bar jumped right ahead with a flicker of the image. The camera time log had skipped all the way forward to 11:57.

Whatever it was, it didn't look good.

There were a number of hypotheses that could have explained the missing footage. After all, it could have been a momentary malfunction, the signal jammed by some electromagnetic disturbance or other, although of course it never was. Her gut feeling was pointing to a very specific moment, the one where the Chief's hand disappeared into his jacket, just before the flicker.

She closed the video and took off her earphones. She couldn't report it to the Chief in case he had something to do with the tampering. Millican was out of the question as he was more likely to dismiss it than accept he had to investigate it.

She had to find out what happened during those twelve missing minutes. If the Chief really was responsible, there were authorities she could talk to, but pointing the finger wasn't going to be enough.

Leaving her desk, Stephanie checked the time. She had another full hour before the meeting. Enough to check in with Steve in the surveillance room. She went by the kitchen to make two coffees, then headed over.

"Fancy some wake-up juice?" she said, leaning against the door jamb, tantalisingly holding up one of the mugs.

Steve was sitting in front of four screens, each one split into four sections, images shifting from one room to another, one corner to another, like a very dull reality television program.

He started in his seat when he heard Stephanie's voice only to rejoice at the sight of coffee. "Oh, yes, I could murder a brew right now. Is it black?"

"Black, two sweeteners."

"You truly are wife material." He took a small sip from the mug she offered him, then winced. "Better let it rest a while," he said, leaving it on the desk to cool. "What can I do for you,

51

Miss Agent Davis?"

"You're not going to drop that, are you?"

"Not until I can call you Mrs Agent Phillips."

She pulled the extra chair from under the desk and sat down next to him. "I'm not marrying your cousin, Steve," she jested. "Now tell me, were you on duty yesterday?"

"For sure, six to midday. Martins and Steele turned the break room into a mini-basketball court. Otherwise, it was a fairly uneventful morning," he confirmed, already moving the live feed to the side to make space for the previous day's recording. "What bits do you need?"

"Interrogation Room 2, make it from 10 a.m."

He selected date and time, and the partitioned room came into view. The angle was the same as the fragmented video she had found. The scene rolled forward, with the Chief entering the room and having a short exchange with Lucy before the screen flickered and a whole twelve minutes went by in a blip.

"That's odd," commented Steve.

"Did any of the other cameras freeze yesterday around that time?"

"No, I don't think so. Then again, halls are pretty dull, Davis. It's not unusual for the screen to look frozen."

"What about the interrogation room? Did you notice any-thing odd during the live feed?"

"No, I mean, the Chief was in that room, so I didn't really pay too much attention, you know," he started explaining.

Stephanie rested a hand on his shoulder. "It's okay, Steve. You did nothing wrong." She then turned to the screen. "Could you get the image from the camera on the other side?"

"The one on the girl's side of the room? Sure."

Steve ticked a couple of boxes and selected a new line from a

52

dropdown menu. The screen blinked. The room looked exactly the same from the other side of the barrier, except the Chief was the blurry figure behind the plastic wall, while Lucy sat at the table, fully in focus, sipping her coffee. Stephanie raised her own mug to take a sip, wincing at the boiling brew.

The scene rolled on as before and, once again, the screen flickered and jumped forward when the Chief reached into his jacket. Twelve minutes later, and he hadn't moved. His hands reappeared from beneath the lapel, empty as it had been twelve minutes earlier.

"I don't understand," said Steve. He rewound the video and watched it again.

Stephanie stared at the screen, not really taking in any of it, her mind already trying to patch the pieces of the puzzle together.

Whatever the Chief had been reaching for in his pocket, it must have been responsible for the glitch. There were a number of gadgets that she knew could have served that purpose. She just had to find proof that that was what was hidden in the Chief's jacket.

A beep from her phone stole her attention away. *Speak of the devil*, she thought. The message was short and straightforward: all questioning suspended until further notice. At that point, she wasn't even surprised.

* * *

During the following days, the Chief kept on denying Stephanie's requests for a meeting. The mission had suddenly turned into a game of waiting for permission to do her job.

Meanwhile, she was aware of a meeting being arranged between Frank and his sister – however that came to be allowed, nobody seemed to know.

When she finally managed to organise a second meeting with Frank, the siblings' reunion had already happened. They had met in a fenced-off part of the courtyard, a mesh fence separating them. There was footage of them standing six feet apart. No audio recording available.

It was just short of twenty-four hours after that when Stephanie made her way into the interrogation room. Frank was already there, pacing nervously on the other side of the plastic barrier. It took him a few seconds before he noticed her, as if he hadn't even heard the door opening when she came in.

"Good morning, Frank."

"Agent Davis," he said. He was evidently trying his best to act casual, but the way he was rubbing the palm of his hands betrayed his nervousness.

"Why don't you drop the Agent. Call me Stephanie," she said in an attempt to make him settle.

It didn't work. He stopped walking only to grab the back of the chair like a buoy in the middle of a stormy sea. "I was wondering, could we talk outside?" A moment of hesitation, then, "Please, Stephanie."

She stopped midway through pulling the chair away from the table. "I suppose that can be arranged," she conceded cautiously. "Do you mind if I ask why?"

"Please," he insisted. "I'd like to be outside."

There was something urgent in his plea. She nodded. "Give me a minute."

Seeking the Chief's approval would've been a waste of time;

- IV -

he had taken the habit of spending his mornings at headquarters, and he still wasn't answering her calls. Instead, she called on Frank's escort and asked to have him brought back to his quarters.

Out of the building, a gale of November wind brushed against her as she wondered if she should have stopped by the office to take her jacket. Too late, anyway. Stephanie took the footpath that led to the field at the back, which coasted the offices and the old barracks. In the closing distance, Frank's small garden was surrounded by a mesh fence that made it look a lot like an enclosure. He was already standing outside wrapped in a brown coat, looking a lot like a meerkat surveying the horizon, and not one bit calmer than he had been in the interrogation room.

She kept her distance from the barrier, though she wondered if her phone would even record a voice from six feet away. "Is this any better?" she asked him, as she prepared to start the recording.

"I don't think you should record this," he said, a hand grasping the fence as if trying to physically prevent her from pressing the record button.

"Care to elaborate?" she asked, her thumb hovering over the screen.

Frank's eyes were wide open, wildly going from the phone to Stephanie. "Hear me out first," he pleaded.

She breathed in, quickly assessing the circumstances, then nodded. Making a show of putting the phone away in the back pocket of her jeans, she brushed the thumb against the surface, hoping she'd hit the right spot, then stepped forward – six-feet distance be damned. She had to give the microphone a fighting chance.

"What is it?" she asked.

55

"My sister is going to take it," he said, words falling out of his mouth. "I don't know how, but she's going to break that thing out of here. That's why they're letting us out early. I could bet my life on it. You have to stop her."

The air seemed to grow colder around Stephanie. First the camera glitch, now this. "Are you talking about the Skaara? Do you think it's controlling her?"

He shook his head. "No, not my sister. I would've noticed." He took half a step left, then right, before coming back to centre, his hands tucked so deeply in his pockets he might have pushed a hole through them.

"That's a heavy accusation. Why would she do that?"

"It's my sister – why does she do anything?" he said with a sneer. It was a rhetorical question, even if Stephanie would have loved to hear Frank's answer. Lucy was opportunistic, not stupid.

"The alien is secured. I've seen it myself. It's not in a position to take over anybody else." She wasn't sure for whose benefit she was saying that – Frank's or her own. There was so much they didn't know about the creature, that it could have been manipulating the entire base without anyone knowing. It could have been manipulating Frank right then.

He clenched his jaw. "What if there's more of them? What if there's another spaceship that you still haven't found? What if they came peacefully, and now we kidnapped one of their own and they take it as an act of war?"

He was right, of course, and he was glaring at her as if she was public enemy number one. Kidnapper of aliens.

"How are you so sure about this?" she asked, bringing the conversation back to his sister and away from interplanetary diplomatic disasters. "Did she tell you about it?"

56

"She didn't have to. They're letting her out tomorrow, apparently, and me too. She didn't say why, but sure it sounded like she was bragging about it. She said she made friends with the right people."

That explained nothing. "Maybe she's cooperating, and the Chief agreed to let her go early. You both seem to be clear of contamination, after all, according to the lab coats."

Frank shook his head. "My sister is not the sort of person who makes friends with your sort of people."

"None taken," commented Stephanie bitterly.

Realising the misstep, Frank rushed to recover. "I'm sorry, I meant no offence."

Stephanie shrugged it off. It still didn't make sense. "Even if she was planning a heist, there's no way she could pull it off. Her room is locked. There are cameras everywhere. There's no way she'd get away with it."

"You don't know my sister."

Stephanie had studied her file and had been given a detailed profile, though. "Unless she can walk through walls, we'll be ready for whatever she's planning."

"What if somebody's helping her from the inside?"

Stephanie pressed her lips tight while part of her brain went on a side quest for worst-case scenarios. There was one particularly realistic that came to mind – the missing footage, the siblings' early release, the Chief's odd behaviour. It all fit together. The only question remaining was Lucy's motive. It was starting to sound like a James Bond film – if James Bond did aliens – but it made general sense.

"Listen," he continued, "maybe I'm being paranoid. Maybe my sister is just sailing her own boat out of here. Or maybe I'm right and that alien thing is taking advantage of her to work its way out. And I don't think you can risk me being right."

"Why are you talking to me about this?" She hadn't meant to ask so bluntly, but it occurred to her that, from his point of view, she must have been as much of a suspect as any other agent in the facility.

He pursued his lips and raised his eyebrows. "It's not like I'm allowed to talk to many people, am I?"

Fair point, she thought, then nodded. "Thank you. For your trust. I will take care of it."

The money tree was looking sorry in the corner of the room. Lucy glanced at the mug of coffee in her hand, then back at the plant. She took a long sip. As she sat down at the table, she rested the mug beside her, hand still loosely wrapped around it.

She had spent the previous week trudging in and out of laboratories, sitting with the psychiatrist and being checked for any kind of contamination. She had come out clean and of sound mind, despite feeling like the exact opposite. At least people had stopped talking to her through either hazmat suits or plastic walls.

She wondered how much of the same thing the Skaara had had to suffer. An odd wave of sympathy mixed with her revulsion for the creeper, almost as if taking it out of there was a good thing to do, morally speaking. That would have been ironic, at least.

Meanwhile, the alien had been true to its word. Cook had arranged for her to meet Frank – even if only for a few minutes and separated by a mesh fence and six feet of empty space – and their quarantine was to be officially rescinded in a matter of hours. Life was good again. Unless something happened to put her back behind a locked door, which was very likely, considering the circumstances.

Absent-mindedly playing with the drawstrings of her hoodie, she realised she had pulled too far when it came out of the hem. She glanced up at the camera while she hid the evidence in the back pocket of her cargo trousers, wondering if she was going to receive a bill for damage.

Lucy's only real worry was for her brother. He hadn't looked too good. His face had been paler than usual, which deepened the black marks under his eyes. As they were talking, he kept rubbing the palm of his hands. He hadn't been sleeping, she was sure of it. His nerves were visibly in shreds.

She took another sip of coffee. Cook was late for their meeting. She didn't mind too much. The idea of that alien nugget piloting his brain still gave her shivers, especially since there was no longer any plastic barrier between them.

She let her mind drift back to Frank.

"What do you think they'll do with it?" he had asked her.

He hadn't meant much by it, yet she recoiled at the question, her voice rising an octave when she replied. "What are you talking about? Who's they?"

What a dumb thing to say. The frown on his face made her worry he might have figured something out. "The government, I guess. Or whoever is supposed to take care of things from outer space."

She had looked away. "Sell it to a circus? How would I know?"

Lucy had never been good at lying to her brother. Even then, she could see he wasn't convinced by her performance. He knew she was up to something. She just hoped he would be clever enough to stay out of it.

She ran her finger around the rim of the mug, a drop of coffee sticking to her thumb. Everything was set for her to leave the facility in the afternoon, Lucy knew that much. No hint on accessing the laboratory, nor on how to get the creeper out without being seen. For a moment, she considered leaving the base and going on her merry way, leaving the alien behind.

No, she couldn't do that. Frank's release had been aptly scheduled to happen two hours after hers, in case she decided to do just that. How clever.

She jumped up from her chair when the door opened, and Edward Cook walked in. A wave of cologne wrapped around her, and she added that to the list of reasons she missed the protection of the plastic wall.

He didn't waste any time on chit chat. He reached inside his jacket for the magic pen, and the cameras clicked into sleep. "Can you drive?" he asked.

"Is that a real question?" she replied with a sneer.

He ignored the remark and threw some car keys at her. Lucy tried to catch them and missed. They bounced against the back of her hand and fell on the table. She raised her eyebrows at him and pretended that was where they were supposed to land all along.

He shrugged. "It's the red Corsa by the entrance."

"I thought you wanted me to be inconspicuous."

"You're expected to leave the base at two in the afternoon. There's no reason to be inconspicuous."

"Except for the part where I don't have a licence," she pointed out. "My entire non-existent driving history is on your record. People will notice."

"Are you able to drive a vehicle?"

Lucy exhaled. What nonsense. "Yes."

"People will not be concerned with your means of transportation so long as you don't do anything suspicious while you leave."

He paused long enough for Lucy to absorb the full scope of the statement. It was a very subtle threat, but a threat, nonetheless.

"Consider the car a parting gift, as a thank you for your cooperation."

"I didn't ask for a car," she retorted.

"You're getting one."

There was nothing she liked about that gift, the colour of the car least of all. The tone of Cook's voice, however, didn't leave much space for negotiation. She picked up the keys and hid them in her trousers pocket. "How am I supposed to get in the lab, anyway? Or do you expect me to improvise that part?"

He took a magnetic pass from his pocket and handed it to her, along with the magic pen. Lucy hesitated. His laid-back attitude was not reassuring – as if he was going to leave her alone in the jungle with a broken jeep and a screwdriver.

She grabbed the pass and the magic pen. If she had to make it out of the jungle, better to have a screwdriver than nothing at all. "Now I really feel like Black Widow in the *Avengers*," she remarked with a smirk. "Are you sure we're going to the landing site? I'm still quite keen on Disneyland."

Disappointingly, Cook ignored her request. "You're taking me back to the spaceship. You'll find a map in the glove compartment of the car. You can use that to find the way."

A screwdriver and a map. What a lucky day. Except she hated maps, at least those on paper. "We had to do that old school, didn't we?"

"The laboratory staff will have a one-hour long lunch at midday. The cage will be unsupervised for that long. The combinations to the three locks are saved in the computer."

"Is there a password to the computer?"

"You should look for a sticky note on the desk."

"One last thing. How do I get out of my room?" she asked. Her release was at two, lunch break was at midday, and the magnetic card was going to do nothing to open her very traditional deadbolt lock.

"I'm sure you can figure something out," he said, then waved at the magnetic badge. "Now put that away and reactivate the cameras."

Lucy glanced at the pen as if it was the One Ring of Sauron. She slid the magnetic card up her sleeve and the pen in trousers' pocket before clicking the cameras to life. When she looked up, all the red lights were flashing again.

As if that was his cue, Edward Cook straightened his tie, then walked to the door. "Good luck," he said, before turning the handle and disappearing down the hall.

It was a handful of seconds before the door opened again. Her escort was ready to take her back to her quarters. Lucy wondered if he had been standing outside, and if he had heard anything. Or maybe that thing had lied to her and was really keeping every single SafeOp agent under mind-control – its very own human army. *No, that wouldn't make sense*, she thought, reining in the galloping paranoia.

"Can I take the coffee with me?" she asked.

The agent shrugged. She picked up the cup with her left hand and felt the magnetic pass slide inside her sleeve, all the way back to her bent elbow. The agent didn't seem to notice anything. So far so good.

Once they reached the door of her room, the agent opened it to let her in. She stepped ahead and held it open, leaning on the doorjamb as she let the magnetic card slide out of her sleeve and onto the chair behind the wall.

"Say, is it really necessary to lock me in again?" she asked with a teasing smile.

"It's procedure. We can't chance you unsupervised around the base."

Clearly. Lucy's hands went to find the door latch, keeping it well hidden behind her back. "There's not much to go sightseeing anyway. It's just a bit depressing to be constantly under lock and key. What time do you reckon I can get out of this hellhole?"

"Schedule says thirteen hundred," he replied stiffly.

Lucy raised an unimpressed eyebrow. "That's one o'clock in the afternoon, for us poor mortals?"

He cleared his throat. "Yes, one o'clock, miss."

She felt the urge to poke him in the ribs at hearing him call her *miss*, but her hands were already busy elsewhere. She was almost done, only needed a few more seconds. Making her best impression of a grateful smile, and a bit of a bow to cover the last effort in her endeavour, she said, "Well, it was lovely meeting you, Mr Bond. I sure hope you won't forget your favourite guest at the SafeOp Resort."

Before he found a suitable comeback to her mockery, she straightened up, closed the door on him and leaned against it, listening as the agent finally walked away. She exhaled when he did, then slowly and silently pulled on the door, opening it a sliver. She had never tried the trick using drawstrings, but there wasn't anything else for her to work with. As she tested the latch with her fingers, she grinned at the result.

The clock ticking on the wall told her it was only minutes to midday. Just enough time to get ready.

Her backpack had reappeared on top of her bed, together with her clothes. It was a large and bulky thing that Matthew gifted

64

her for her birthday a few months earlier, in preparation for a season full of hikes – his favourite thing and her greatest nightmare. She had managed to avoid most of his attempts, until that very last one, just in time to be cursed with the discovery of an alien spaceship.

She took out the empty metallic water flask, the various maps that Frank had made her carry, and a waterproof kit two sizes too large.

The only items left in the backpack were her phone's USB charger cable, her wallet, and her keys, with the pink sloth still dangling from the keyring. Her phone was still locked in a drawer at reception, waiting for her to collect it on the way out – assuming there was time before they called a red alert on the missing alien creeper.

After quickly changing into her own clothes – freshly washed and ironed, how thoughtful – she took the magic pen out to examine it. There were two small buttons: a green one and a red one. Without an instruction manual, Lucy had no better option than to chance it. She pulled the door open just enough to slide the pen through, then clicked the red button.

When she glanced at the cameras in the closest corner of the hall, the red light had disappeared. Lucy allowed herself a moment of silent excitement before picking up the backpack, sliding the magnetic card in her pocket, and making her way out the door.

There was that familiar thrill in walking down corridors she wasn't supposed to, not too different from sneaking around people's houses after dark. She went cautiously, listened for voices, and carefully deactivated every camera before turning any corner.

There didn't seem to be many people around at all. The few

times she crossed paths with someone, she managed to get away by avoiding eye contact and confidently pretending to belong there just as much as they were. Even then, she kept a quick pace down the same corridors that so many times led her to tedious encounters with the local scientists.

Soon she found herself in front of the door to the science department. A grey box to the left invited her to scan her pass. She hovered the plastic card in front of it and watched the light go from red to green as the door clicked open. She gripped the handle and pulled just enough to let the pen through, then clicked the cameras into sleep.

She had never been in the same room as the Skaara. Her visits had always been limited to the four doors that opened on the left side of the corridor. Those were the laboratories dedicated to the humans. The double door at the end of the hall, however, was the one she was looking for, aptly covered with warning signs like only the best cartoon shows knew how to do.

She stood for a moment in the eerie atmosphere of the empty space, until the loud clang of the closing door shook her back to the present. As the echo reverberated down the hall, Lucy held her breath, listening for anybody on their way to check on the uninvited guest.

The hall remained silent. Lucy slowly exhaled and walked on. Two large signs, one on each side of the double door, warned her she would be exposed to a biological hazard and extra-terrestrial contamination. She tried to peer through the cardboard, to see what was inside, but something was covering the glass on the other side.

To the right of the door, another grey box greeted her with a green light when she presented the magnetic pass. Lucy pulled the handle and deactivated the cameras inside the lab, then walked in.

She remembered the Skaara as a slithery, scaly thing, like a snake that had stolen a spider's legs.

Lucy lowered herself to be level with it. Looking at it, curled up in the corner of its transparent triple-glazed prison, she realised it was way smaller than she expected, and that there was nothing scaly about it. Instead, a few sparse hairs covered its body, just enough to remind her of a terrier with alopecia – except this one had gone almost entirely bald, showing the scratches and marks that all the scientific poking of the previous two weeks had left.

Try as she might, she could not locate the eyes. It gave her the creeps. "I'd say you look pretty, my little space crawler, but even I can't lie in front of this," she muttered. "No offence, of course. Just fact."

She moved her attention to the cage. The Skaara was located inside three boxes, one inside the other, each one kept shut with a combination lock. She surveyed the room and counted three computers on three different desks. Anyone of them could be the one storing the combination, provided she could find the right sticky note with the right password to log in. *Great way to waste some time*, she thought.

She leaned on the table to stand back up, then went to examine the desks. One of them was so clean and tidy it clearly had never been used. The second one had been decorated with a plastic cactus and a framed picture, but had no paper left around, and no sticky note attached anywhere.

The third desk was a complete mess. Bits of paper were scattered everywhere, some of which were clearly irrelevant, while others could have been either notes in some incomprehensible technical lingo, or a particularly elaborate password. It felt like a nightmarish puzzle to solve. Lucy sighed and threw her head back, eyes closed, half hoping all that chaos would dissolve once she opened them again.

"You're not going to help me, are you?" she called to the room, as if the space crawler could have talked back.

In opening her eyes again, she noticed a yellow strip sticking out of the back of one of the screens. "Bingo," she whispered.

She jiggled the mouse, and the computer screen came to life. The username was already selected, so she only needed to cross her fingers and type in the password. A few seconds later, she was looking at the desktop screen. Victory.

The bottom right corner of the screen told her it was just twenty past twelve. She had to be out of there before the whole science crew came back, so she'd better hurry.

A quick look at the document files gave her a whole folder called *Skaara*. "I guess Hairy Spider Snake didn't cut it as a code name."

Inside the folder, amongst all sorts of spreadsheets and reports, she found a simple file note called *pw*. Somebody in that lab didn't have a great imagination when it came to file names. Lame, but useful to Lucy at least.

The note gave her all the combinations she needed. She scribbled them down and was about to turn off the computer when something occurred to her.

From her backpack, she took out her keys and twisted the head of the fluffy sloth to reveal the flash drive. *No one can know when a load of intel about an alien invader might come in handy*, she thought as she plugged the flash drive into the USB port. Estimated download time: five minutes. She could work with that.

Leaving the computer to take care of that, Lucy turned to

- v -

the cage. The space crawler was still curled up in the corner, utterly undisturbed. She took that as a good sign and got to work on the locks. A few attempts later she had managed to open two of the three cages, while the Skaara remained curled up in the opposite corner of the box. It was almost insulting how unperturbed it looked.

As she grabbed the last lock, Lucy had to pause. She couldn't pretend that the lump in her throat was mere excitement. She was terrified. The moment she opened that lock, there was nothing preventing the that thing from jumping on her.

She took a deep breath. Her hands stopped shaking. It was going to be fine. She knew what she was doing – or at least she thought so.

She took off her backpack and opened it, keeping it ready by her side. The last combination opened the last lock. Even if she couldn't see its eyes, Lucy was sure the Skaara's full attention was on her.

"Hear me now, space crawler," she said. "I'm helping you, and I'm doing it of my own free will. If you try any of your mind tricks on me, I swear I'll roast you for dinner. Understood?"

She didn't expect the alien to understand any of it – she had said it more for her own reassurance – yet the creature moved for the first time in response to it. The space crawler crawled tighter on itself, then settled down again. Lucy decided to take that as a yes.

She opened the door and held the open backpack right against the opening. She tried her best to keep steady, while her hands grew sweaty and trembling. "Now come in here."

She peered from behind the open bag and watched the creature as it slowly picked itself up and crawled into the backpack. It looked shorter than she remembered. She cringed

69

at the idea of the missing bit nested in the back of Cook's neck.

Shrugging the thought away, she focused on the task at hand, trying not to think about what monster she was carrying, and what could potentially be unleashed on the world if anything went wrong. It was going to be okay, she repeated to herself. She only had to get out of there and stay in the clear until Frank was safely out. After that, it was a free-for-all. Who knew, she could even get twice the reward for bringing the wretched thing to the actual police. Yes, she knew what she was doing. Probably.

She closed the bag, then swung it on her shoulders. As she did that, a stab of pain somewhere behind her tenth rib made her wince. She took a deep breath and straightened up, waiting for the pain to subside. She had to find some pain killers as soon as she got out of there.

On the computer screen, the download was already at eighty percent and inching its way along the progress bar. The clock was getting closer to twenty to one – so much for a five-minute download time.

As she watched the numbers changing on the screen, Lucy tried not to think about what would happen if anyone walked in before she could get out. She glanced around for cover, but there were very few corners to hide behind. Then she noticed a couple of white lab coats hanging by the door, right next to a box of safety glasses and surgical masks. She grabbed the whole kit and covered up as much as she could. Not perfect, but it could buy her some time.

When the percentage finally reached one hundred, she snatched the flash drive and shoved it into the pocket of the backpack, then made her way into the corridor, holding the door as it closed, so that it lightly clicked instead of booming shut. She exhaled in relief – one moment too early.

At the other end of the hall, the main door unlocked.

"Shit," she murmured as she threw out the magnetic pass to reopen the double door and hide herself behind it. Even wearing the full lab attire, better not chance it.

She listened carefully, trying to guess where the steps were heading, but the door was blocking all noise from coming through.

There was a small window on the door, covered with some paper – disclaimers and warnings about how to get out of there in case something went boom. She ripped one of them away and peered through the plexiglass.

Two men in white coats were walking down the hall. Both were laughing, taking their time before getting back to work. One of them used his badge to open one of the doors, and they were about to walk in when his colleague held him by the arm.

They exchanged a few words, then turned to the double door at the end of the hall. They couldn't see Lucy from that distance, she was sure, but she jerked away from the window just in case. She counted to three, then looked again. The two men were still standing in the hall. Finally, they shrugged and walked into the laboratory, closing the door behind them.

Lucy opened the heavy door once again, her face fully covered by safety goggles and a surgical mask. She walked out and sneaked past the laboratory, hiding the backpack under the lab coat, and hoping nobody was going to come close enough to figure out her disguise. She only had to get to the main corridor, then any half-baked excuse was going to be enough to keep her in the clear.

The twenty yards to get there felt as long as a football field.

She made it to the door and opened it a sliver to glance outside.

There was only one person in sight, and she was standing by the corner, looking the other way.

Lucy slipped out, holding the door as it closed and letting it gently shut, while quickly taking off her disguise and throwing it in the corner. The noise the goggles made when hitting the floor caught the woman's attention.

"Oh, deary me, are you alright?"

"I think so," replied Lucy, sporting her most helpless face. "I lost my escort, though. Would you know how to get to the reception area?"

The woman squinted at her yet seemed to buy Lucy's story. "Honey, you've got more than a few wrong turns! Bit careless of you, to lose your escort like that, isn't it? I'd take you to the reception myself, but there seems to be some commotion on the training grounds on the lake side of the compound. I have to dash, really!"

In spite of that, she thought about it for a moment, then went on to volunteer a detailed series of directions to get Lucy to reception.

Lucy listened carefully, and even managed to keep her mouth shut when she mistook a right turn for a left one. At the end, she politely thanked her and got on her way, slowly and steadily. After all, it wasn't like she was running away or anything. As Cook pointed out, she was scheduled for release.

Whatever the commotion was on the training grounds, Cook must have orchestrated it to get everyone out of her way. How sweet of him.

It felt as if the worst was past her. The silence in the halls told her Cook's diversion had worked, and nobody had yet figured out that the alien had disappeared. Even so, each corner she turned she met with a different white coat walking back to the laboratory. It would be minutes, maybe only seconds before one of them opened the double doors and found the empty cage.

Lucy quickened her pace on the last stretch of corridor.

When she finally reached the reception area, a tinge of panic caught her as she spotted the metal detector by the exit. It wasn't the scanner that worried her so much as the bag search that generally went with it. If Cook had arranged something for her to get past it, she hadn't been told.

She threw the magic pen in a nearby potted plant, then approached the desk. "Hi, I'm Lucy Campbell, checking out."

The woman behind the desk looked up with a frown, then stretched to check the way Lucy had come from. She wasn't satisfied with what she saw. "You should've been escorted here," she remarked, her hand threateningly moving towards the alarm trigger on her desk.

"Something about a commotion on the training grounds? He left me by the door over there." Lucy pointed in the general direction of the rest of the building. "He reckoned I'd be fine the rest of the way, seeing that I'm leaving this place anyway."

The receptionist's hand was lingering on the button. It was as if a human lie-detector was studying Lucy's face for a long moment. Lucy held her gaze, showing off her innocence, while internally twitching to get out of there.

Eventually, the woman checked the day's schedule, pulled her arm back from the alarm button, and relaxed on her chair, shoulders sagging in disappointment. "You'll still need to go through the metal detector over there," she said, nodding at the security agent by the main door. The security agent nodded back. She then took a plastic bag from a drawer and handed it over together with a clipboard. "Your phone. Sign the release paper."

Lucy took the clipboard. A pen was tied to it with a string. "Would you know when my brother, Frank Campbell, is due to be released?" she asked while scribbling her name at the bottom of the page.

"I am not at liberty to disclose that information." The way she said it, the woman could have passed for a robot.

Lucy held her breath – and her temper – for a second. "I'm his sister. His next of kin. We're going to eat together tonight. I just want to know what time to expect him."

"Fifteen hundred hours," the woman replied, then reached out to take the clipboard back. "Thank you."

Challenging her was going to be a waste of time, though Lucy died to break that clipboard on her face. She grabbed the plastic bag instead, then made her way to the metal detector. Together with the plastic bag, her wallet and keys went in the tray by the side, while she swung the backpack over her shoulder and walked gingerly through before the security agent could make a grab for her bag.

All was silent as she stepped across.

"Hold on," said the agent, checking the side of the metal detector. "I don't think this thing is working." He turned to the woman at reception. "Marion, would you give a call to the tech team? This bloody thing has stopped working."

While Marion got on the phone, he reached out a hand, expecting Lucy to hand over the backpack. She knew what was going to happen. It was obvious, really. He was going to open the backpack and give the space crawler the chance to get all touchy-feely with yet another human. She did her best to hide the bout of nausea that hit her at the mere thought.

She kept her gaze right ahead as he ran a portable detector along her body. It was nerve-wracking, even when she knew she had nothing on her that could trigger it. And indeed, the racket stayed silent.

Next was the backpack. Lucy wondered if the little crawler even knew what was happening. With some luck, the agent was going to be satisfied with the silent approval of the portable detector and let her go. Unfortunately, a loud beeping indicated that one of the pockets had something to hide.

He threw a suspicious look at her, while he opened the zipper and reached inside to take out the fluffy pink sloth.

Of course, Lucy thought. *It must have fallen off the keys.* She didn't know how she hadn't noticed it before. That wasn't good. A plush toy wasn't supposed to trigger a metal detector.

The agent was turning the sloth in his hand. He tried the metal detector on the sloth – with loud beeping results – and again on the backpack – where the detector remained silent.

"Is this a toy?" he asked.

She took a deep breath. "A keyring," she explained, nodding towards the tray where her keys were. "It must have come off the bunch."

He held the sloth by one of its arms and lifted it up. He was grinning. Lucy was terrified.

"Marion," he called. "Look at this weeny thing. It's a freaking sloth! A pink one!"

Lucy tried to smile.

Marion burst out laughing. "You're kidding! It looks like the one Scott's daughter has."

It was an inside joke, then. Brilliant. Lucy realised her hand was clenching the rim of the plastic box. She didn't even remember when she had grabbed it in the first place. She forced herself to relax her grip.

The security agent focused on her. "May I ask, where did you get it?"

This was becoming unbearable. She almost wished they would just find the alien and get it over with. "I don't know. My brother got it for me years ago," she managed instead.

"What a funny little thing," he said, squinting at it, as if he was looking at a miniature crypto puzzle. Then his eyes locked onto something. "There you go. The ring. That's what set off the alarm."

He handed the flash drive back to Lucy, who was staring at him with wide eyes, trying to remember how breathing worked. The ring. It took her a second to understand. "Of course, because it's a keyring. There's a ring. A metal one. Right."

She shoved the sloth in her pocket before anybody could take another look at it. She was about to swing the backpack on her shoulder and take that out of danger too when the agent gently pulled it away from her and went to open the zip of the main pocket. "What you got in here?" he asked.

"Nothing much," she said. *Just an alien creature I stole from your laboratory.*

He looked, then reached inside, arm deep in her backpack up to his elbow. Lucy shuddered. That was a lot of hugging surface he was gifting to the space crawler in there.

The agent kept that position for a few long seconds before closing the backpack and handing it back to her. As he did, there was something different about his smile, a sort of emptiness behind it. "Don't know what that bag's made of, but it sure is heavier than it looks," he commented.

Lucy's heart caught in her throat. "Yes," she mumbled. "It's a heavy fabric."

"Well, you're good to go. Stay safe out there."

Lucy closed the backpack that the agent had left open, then

swung it around and over her shoulder. She scurried out of the building before the alien spell had time to wear off.

- VI -

She had half expected Lucy to run off with the bounty in the middle of the night. Frank's suspicion had taken hold of Stephanie, and she had ended up staying at the base as late as she could, watching the security cameras like a boring reality show. Present at the party was also the recording of her conversation with Frank, which sounded surprisingly clear when blasted at full volume in her ears, and the science report.

The last one was the most disappointing. According to the lab coats, the most effective way to fully counteract the Skaara's control was by taking benzodiazepine at a dosage that roughly translated into knocking yourself unconscious. Not massively useful.

Even when she finally went home, Stephanie left the security agent with the instruction to call her directly should anything look less than perfect. She had slept fully dressed, waiting for the phone to ring. When morning came, however, all was quiet. No missed phone calls, and no messages.

On the way out of her flat, Stephanie's eyes fell on her handgun. She had left it on the coffee table when she got back from the Highlands and hadn't picked it up since. She clipped the holster to her belt and appreciated the weight of the gun on her hip. She wasn't going to need it, she decided. Still, better to be safe than sorry.

All was running regularly at the base when she arrived. The Skaara was still safely locked in its glass cage, and Lucy and Frank's dismissal was planned for the afternoon, two hours apart from one another.

She made her way to the security room. The agent on duty that morning was a blond moustachioed man by the name of Briggs, with the kind of frowning smile that ended in a shake of his head. She sat to watch the cameras with him, resting the handgun on the table in front of her together with the customary dark brew.

Briggs looked at the weapon with surprised eyebrows. "Surveillance is rarely that exciting, you know?" he said with a chuckle and a shake of the head.

"Wanna bet?" she replied.

They sat in silence for the better part of two hours, until Stephanie's phone rang in her pocket. It was the Chief. "Your report is not on my desk," he said right away.

"A few points needed clarification. It will be in your inbox by midday today," she replied promptly.

"What points?" he asked. His tone was suddenly alarmed.

"Some confused statements," she offered. "They're likely fabrications, but I can't write them off as fantasy without having a proper look."

There was a pause, then the Chief said, "No later than one o'clock."

After ending the call, Stephanie exhaled and leaned back on the chair, eyes back on the screens.

Briggs had caught on to her tone in the brief exchange. "Trouble?"

"As if I could tell you about it."

79

Briggs tutted and glanced sideways at her. "Aren't you bored of this already?"

"Not if it's worth the wait," she replied. In truth, she was struggling to keep her mind focused.

"How about some coffee, then?" he offered.

She smiled. "You need to ask?" As Briggs made to stand, she held his shoulder down. "Let me get it. You watch the screens."

She picked up the gun and clipped it back on. It was only going to take a few minutes, and she needed to stretch her legs anyway. It also gave her time to think about what to do with the Chief. If she was wrong, as she hoped she was, then she just had to send in the partial report she had already prepared and dismiss Frank's story as the reveries of a traumatised mind.

If she was right, on the other hand, the planet was on the verge of a potential alien invasion. A thought like that would have been comical, if it wasn't horrifyingly plausible. The mere thought sounded almost comical.

She walked back to the surveillance room with a mug in each hand. "Anything fun happen while I was gone?"

"That all depends on your definition of fun," he replied, taking one of the mugs. "They went to get the girl."

Stephanie froze halfway through the motion of placing her gun back on the table. "Get her and take her where?"

"Interrogation room three," he replied, clicking something on the computer screen to bring one of the camera views to the foreground.

It was one of the smallest interrogation rooms, with no partitions and only one camera angle, the one that was facing Lucy, who was sitting at the table, a mug of coffee between her hands.

Stephanie sat on the edge of her chair, leaning forward, her face inches from the screen and the gun cradled in her lap. She started when Lucy suddenly stood up – the Chief had entered the room.

"Bit edgy, are we?" commented Briggs, shaking his moustache in a smile while carefully eyeing the gun.

Stephanie purposefully ignored him. "Can you add the audio?"

He shook his head. "Sorry, mate. There's no live feed in room three. You'll have to ask for the recording later."

She sat back. Short of walking into the room and demanding to know what they were talking about, she had no choice but to wait and observe. Both Lucy and the Chief were impressively still. He was only visible from his left shoulder angle, but Cook's position looked odd even from there. His left arm was bent at the elbow, as if he were pointing at something – or stuck in the process of taking something from under the lapel of his jacket. Everything on screen looked just as still as he was. Including the time.

"He's doing it again," she murmured, clipping the gun back on her belt, ready to leave and catch him in the act. That was when some static ran through the screen, a glitch that made the image waver for a second, and the clock resumed ticking.

The Chief's position had changed, with both arms down at his sides. He stood like that for a moment before he straightened his tie and walked out.

A handful of seconds, then the door opened again. As Lucy stood up to meet her escort, something caught Stephanie's eye.

"Briggs, can you rewind that?" she asked.

"Sure, to when?"

"Just fifteen seconds or so."

The timer rolled back thirty seconds. Stephanie leaned even

81

closer to the screen, watched the screen glitch once more, then Lucy stood up from her chair, and it was there in her pocket – the interference pen. So that was how he had jammed the signal.

She stood up, ready to leave. "Shit," she murmured.

Briggs hadn't caught any of that. "What? What happened?"

"Nothing, all good," she lied. "Can you check that Miss Campbell is back at her quarters?"

Briggs moved a few screens and brought up the live feed of the corridor that led to Lucy's room. All was empty and quiet.

"Keep me posted. I've got to go."

She left before Briggs could say anything else, rushing to catch Lucy before she had time to slip away. As soon as she reached the stairs, however, the Chief's voice called her back.

"Davis, a word."

Stephanie stopped and turned. She hadn't noticed him standing there.

She covered the distance and forced herself to focus on him, instead of checking the halls. "Sir, it's good to see you at the base."

He ignored the comment. "Walk with me, would you?"

It was a trick, clear as day. He was taking her further away from Lucy's quarters, and in the opposite direction from the science department, yet Stephanie had no choice but to follow.

"I've heard you pushed it to midnight yesterday. Is there anything I should be aware of?" He didn't sound worried.

She had never cared for lying, especially to him. It made her skin itch. He was the only person she ever felt she could trust, after the last one shot her and shoved her in the boot of the car. Maybe because of the way Frank had brought up that metaphor, she couldn't stop thinking about it, and the potential for history to repeat itself.

She avoided looking at him as they walked. "Just following up from the interview with Frank, sir. He had some funny ideas about the Skaara that I wanted to check on."

"I suppose I'll read all about them in the report," he replied. "How are you today?"

"I'm very well, sir."

The Chief shook his head. "The dark circles under your eyes tell a different story. We need you – I need you – fresh and rested when you're on duty, understood?"

That was a most uncharacteristic speech, not to mention slightly uncomfortable. Stephanie tried to hide her puzzlement. "Yes, sir."

He slowly nodded, stood silent for a moment, then dismissed her and walked away in silence.

He had been stalling her. Yes, the Chief had always had a shine for her, but that had too much of a paternalistic feeling to be genuine.

She made an effort not to run on the way to Lucy's quarters. When she arrived in front of the door, she took a breath and pulled out her gun. The door oscillated backwards when she knocked. She pushed it open into an empty room. That was not good.

If an escort had come to pick her up, there was a chance Lucy was still under surveillance. Stephanie caught her breath before her gaze fell on the lock.

A drawstring was stuck inside the slot, keeping the lock from clicking shut. That was how she had done it. Stephanie had to admit, she was impressed.

Gun back in its holster, she marched her way to the laboratories while dialling for the surveillance room on her phone.

"Miss me already?" said Briggs as he picked up.

She ignored that. "Do you have a visual of the science department?"

"I have a visual of everything, Davis," he replied. "Laboratories are empty."

Not reassuring. She picked up her pace. "What do you mean, *empty*?"

"I mean all white coats are on lunch break. It's a desolated country down there."

If Lucy was using the interference pen, those labs were going to look like a desolated country for a long while. "Thank you, Briggs."

She hung up and made her way to the science department – or at least she would have, if she hadn't crashed into someone at the first corner she turned.

"Oh, thank goodness I found you," the obstacle said. Victoria was standing in the middle of the way, holding onto Stephanie's arm as if her life depended on it. "There's a major commotion going on. We need your help!"

"What commotion? What happened?"

"No time for that! Follow me!" And with the last exclamation mark, she was already rushing down the hall, dragging Stephanie with her.

The Skaara must have been taken already. If somebody had spotted Lucy and raised the alarm, maybe there was still a chance to catch her.

"Evans, where are we going?" Stephanie asked.

"This way!" she replied, then dashed forward.

Not very descriptive. The last door in front of them was the one leading outside to the grounds on the Blagdon side – basically a large green expanse that used to be the training

84

grounds, followed by a row of houses looking onto Blagdon Lake further ahead. Not the smartest way to go, unless Lucy was up for a long hike.

After flinging the door open, Victoria still didn't stop to explain. "There!" she said, pointing at something in the distance, then retreated and closed the door behind her, effectively locking Stephanie out of that side of the building. Splendid.

In the direction Victoria had pointed, three SafeOp agents were already making their way back. Stephanie recognised a few of them. Hopefully, they were going to make more sense than Victoria had.

"Agent Murray," she called. "What's going on here? What was the commotion?"

"Nothing to report, Davis. False alarm," he grunted back. "And what the hell are you doing here anyway?"

That wasn't right. "Evans called me here. She said there was a commotion," she explained.

Murray laughed at that. "Since when do you concern yourself with trespassing civilians, big shot?" he taunted. Murray had never been her best friend and didn't miss any opportunity to show it. "You need to change your PA if she wastes your time like that."

"Not my PA, Murray. Now stop being a dick," she shot back. "Are you sure it was just civilians trespassing?"

He locked his jaw and stared right through her. "That's what I said."

Shit. Stephanie sprinted away and circled the building to the closest entrance, vaguely aware of Murray's voice shouting his requests for explanations. She didn't have time to debrief. By then, Lucy had likely already gotten the Skaara out of its cage.

Rushing down halls and stairs, she finally arrived at the

science department, where she soon realised she was too late. A young technician was rushing out of the Skaara's double door. He almost crashed into Stephanie, eyes opened so wide they threatened to fall off his face.

"Gwyn. Gwyn is gone," he kept repeating.

He careened down the hall, half crashing and half pushing the door open, barely remembering to scan his pass on his way out.

Lucy was likely on her way out. The alarm should have been ringing around the base already. Stephanie dialled the Chief. "The Skaara has left the cage. Should we raise the alarm?"

There was a short pause, then he replied, "Thank you, Davis. I expect you to find her."

He hung up before she could say anything. He hadn't sounded surprised, nor worried. It vaguely smelled like a trap. The Chief had been playing her the whole morning.

Once again, Stephanie dialled for Briggs.

"Are you going to ask me about the girl?" he said right away.

"Where is she?"

"Reception, checking out as expected," he said dismissively. "Anything I should be aware of?"

She hesitated. "Keep an eye on her for me."

She quickened her steps towards the reception area. In spite of the panic in the laboratory, the rest of the base looked unaffected – or at least that was what Stephanie thought before spotting a group of four agents, geared up and rushing out to the courtyard. She turned another corner, and another squad rushed past her. The alarm had been raised but only as a decoy. With everyone checking the grounds on the other side, nobody would be left to secure the entrance.

When Stephanie turned the corner to the reception area, the

emptiness hit her like a punch. She jogged up to the desk. "Miss Lucy Campbell – has she gone already?" she asked, her fingers tapping in urgency.

The receptionist looked at her sideways. "Just about, yes."

She rushed to the entrance door and looked out at the parking lot. A red Vauxhall Corsa was leaving by the front gate. She made a mental note of the registration plate, then checked the rest of the vehicles parked there, locking on a black Kawasaki, the helmet hanging by the side of the seat.

She rushed behind the reception desk, amidst the woman's protests. She spotted what was clearly a motorbike key strapped to a Kawasaki keyring. "Make a note, I'm taking this. I'll bring it back in a minute."

The only security agent in the room raised his hand. "It's mine, actually."

"Yeah? Nice ride," she said absent-mindedly, circling back round the desk and heading out.

With Lucy only seconds ahead, Stephanie quickly turned on the engine, pulled the bike upright, and soon was opening the throttle and crossing the gate. It was indeed a sweet ride. Too bad it was only going to be for a few minutes.

The road leaving the base was a narrow and winding stretch of asphalt, which only joined the regular traffic a short mile ahead. Her mind focused solely on the road, Stephanie pushed the bike as fast as it was safe to do so. When she finally caught a glance of the red Corsa in the distance, Lucy was preparing to turn left at the crossroads. By the time Stephanie had reached the intersection herself, the distance between them had shortened to a few yards.

The road she turned into was straight and clear – ideal conditions.

Overtaking the red Corsa was a matter of seconds. Stephanie brought the bike to a stop with a screech of the tyres, parking it sideways across the road. She had just enough time to take off her helmet and prod the bike on the kickstand before the car screeched to a halt a few yards away. She threw the helmet to the side and took out the gun, keeping it lowered, waiting.

It was possible Lucy hadn't seen the gun at all. Stephanie saw her hand move from the steering wheel to some place behind the dashboard – the gearbox, she realised. She was going to reverse and head away in the opposite direction. Turning the car around wasn't going to be an easy manoeuvre in the narrow space. Lucy couldn't really believe she could get away with it.

Leaving the safety on, Stephanie pointed the gun straight at her, hoping the girl would get the hint before she had to use it. If she didn't, she could always shoot at the tyres. It would make a hell of a noise, but it would also prevent her from driving away.

Then the Skaara. She couldn't know yet how much of a threat the alien could be, if it was busy controlling the girl, or if she was acting of her own free will instead.

Meanwhile, Lucy was still sitting in the car, seemingly wondering what to do.

When the girl's hand started moving slowly back to the steering wheel, Stephanie allowed herself to exhale.

Weapon steady on target, Stephanie gestured for Lucy to get out of the vehicle. She was horribly aware of the fact that they were standing in the middle of a public road. The closest house was too far to care, yet anybody could drive by at any moment. Cyclists loved that route. It was sheer luck that nobody showed up.

Nobody. Not even backup.

Lucy stepped out of the car, her hands raised above her head in a mock gesture of surrender that her expression alone did enough to contradict.

Stephanie moved a couple of steps closer. "Who am I talking to, Lucy or the Skaara?"

The girl chuckled. "I'm the spirit of Christmas Future. Don't you recognise me?"

Stephanie lowered her gun. There she was, Lucy Campbell, in all her sarcastic glory.

"What, forgot to bring your licence to kill?" the girl teased.

Stephanie wasn't as keen on banter. "Where's the Skaara?"

"Is that what you call it?"

"It's what it calls itself, didn't you know that? I thought you two were friends."

The smirk on Lucy's face turned into a grimace, even if for just a split second. "And I thought you didn't have a sense of humour. Colour me impressed."

"Where is it, Campbell?"

"Guess," she replied, then threw a quick glance sideways, which Stephanie followed straight to the passenger seat and the backpack that Lucy had left there. "Be my guest. I'm thinking the army might like to meet her."

No, Stephanie wasn't going to fall for it. "Nice try," she said, raising the gun and pointing it at Lucy once again. "Give me the keys of the car and get back inside."

"Oh, fuck no."

Lucy lashed forward before Stephanie could realise what was happening. The surprise was enough for the girl to grab the gun and push it upwards towards the sky.

It was a clumsy attempt.

Careful not to misfire, Stephanie leveraged Lucy's shoulder

89

and wrapped her in a chokehold.

"Well, look at that," teased Lucy, her voice strained. "Who knew Cook had such well-trained watchdogs?"

No witticism was going to get her out of there, though. Stephanie kept her hold tight around the girl's neck, blocking the windpipe and interrupting the blood flow to her head. Soon enough, Lucy's arms stopped flapping around ineffectively and dropped to the side.

Propping the girl's body against hers, Stephanie loosened the chokehold and took a deep breath, then, with some effort, she held the girl with one arm while re-holstering the gun. Thankful that the door of the car had remained open, she lowered Lucy onto the driver's seat, then slipped the girl's legs under the steering wheel and took the keys from the ignition. As she did that, a pink ball of fur caught her eye.

It was sitting in the cup holder, left there like an afterthought. It looked like nothing more than a plush toy, except the head was turned the wrong angle. When she picked it up, she felt the presence of a harder skeleton inside. She twisted the head, and it popped off to reveal a flash drive underneath. How smart.

Maybe it was nothing, or maybe it was everything. She pocketed it, then locked Lucy inside the car. As she did that, her phone started ringing. When she picked up, the Chief's voice came through the speaker. "Did you get it?"

"The thief is in custody. I'm going to request backup before potential contact with the second subject, sir."

That was half a lie. There was no one she could call for backup without getting local authorities involved. No one apart from the Chief, that was.

"Backup, yes," he repeated. The words were encouraging. The tone wasn't. "Do you have eyes on the Skaara?"

90

Stephanie looked at the backpack. She had assumed the alien was inside. Lucy had hinted at it when she had asked. If it was waiting anywhere else in the car, however, there was a risk the backup team would get blindsided, and the last thing they needed was for the Skaara to have its own personal action team.

She walked her way to the passenger door. "Not yet, sir. Most likely scenario, the subject was carried inside the backpack."

"We don't work on scenarios, Davis. Secure the vehicle and sit tight. Backup is on its way."

The call dropped before she could protest.

It was a trap, there was no question about it. She had to get ready, minimise the risk – if that was even possible.

A quick inspection told her the Skaara wasn't hiding inside the vehicle, nor in the boot, and even the engine looked clear.

Lucy was still unconscious in the driver's seat. Not that she would be much of a threat, but Stephanie couldn't risk her waking up and give her another alien minion to worry about. She took the security straps she found on the motorbike to tie Lucy's hands to the steering wheel, knot on the underside, in case she woke up and tried to free herself. Closing the door, she locked the car once again. The first part was done.

It was then that the Chief's car showed up. He parked just behind Lucy's and walked up to her. He was alone.

"Are we expecting a team, sir?" she asked, although she already knew the answer.

"We have to minimise human exposure to the Skaara," he said, his eyes unfocused, looking right past her. "After all, it can only control one human at a time. If Gwyn gets hold of you, I shall be backup enough."

Stephanie didn't know which was the creepiest – the fact that he called people *humans* or that he called the alien *Gwyn*.

She had to think fast. "May I suggest I might be your backup in this case? After all, I'm the one with the gun."

She unholstered her weapon as she said that. This time, she took the safety off. She didn't want to shoot the Chief – not after everything he had done for her – but an alien-controlled version of him was a whole different discussion.

"Where is it?" he asked after a moment.

"The backpack is in the passenger seat," she replied, "The girl is tied to the steering wheel. She won't be a problem."

He nodded, then spent a few seconds staring at the car. It wasn't long, yet it felt weird how he just stood still, gazing ahead, as if he could see the backpack through the metal. Finally, he ordered, "Unlock the door."

Grateful for remote technology, Stephanie took her place just past the side mirror and readied her gun, then pushed the button to unlock the car. The Chief went to open the passenger door. That gave her perfect cover, while she still had a clear view of the front seat.

She could feel the adrenaline level rising, every muscle ready to go, her mind sharp and focused. That was it, she knew it. Save the world or spell its doom. No pressure.

The Chief carefully approached the backpack. It was the kind that closed with a zip across the top, which made it impossible to open it without getting dangerously close, yet he didn't look too worried about it.

He gently pulled the slider open a few inches. Stephanie stepped aside to get a better visual.

The backpack remained quiet. It was possible the Skaara wasn't in there after all.

"Come and stand behind me." There was urgency in the Chief's tone.

Maybe she had misunderstood his intentions after all. Maybe he hadn't been aiding the alien's escape at all. It wouldn't have been the first time he ran a mission on a need-to-know basis and kept her in the dark about most details. Although this time his behaviour had been exceptionally odd.

She moved to stand behind him as instructed, weapon aimed straight at the top of the bag, where she expected the Skaara to appear.

The Chief slowly pulled the zip wide open. Still nothing happened.

"This will be enough," he said as he stood up and backed away, leaving Stephanie fully exposed.

No, that wasn't right. She had no time to make sense of it, though. The backpack moved ever so slightly, and she barely stopped herself from shooting it right then.

A moment later, she wished she had.

She had never expected the Skaara to be that fast.

The sound of the gun going off was the last thing she heard before everything went dark.

- VII -

Lucy could hear rain tapping on the glass overhead. How lovely. Just like when she was a little girl. She would leave her bedroom in the middle of the night to sleep in the loft instead. She did it for the rain, to hear its tapping noise against the skylight.

She inhaled the dusty smell. It wasn't what the loft used to smell like, and the air was colder than she remembered. She shivered in her seat – quite uncomfortable, albeit being better than lying on the thin carpet in the corner of the roof. She couldn't remember bringing an armchair up there, though.

Her eyelids felt like they had been glued closed. The dull, pervasive hum in her head exploded in an intense wave of pain as soon as she tried to lift her neck upright. She held her breath for a moment – as if that would make it go away. When she finally opened her eyes, her own hands were the first thing she saw. They were tied to the steering wheel with some black straps.

"Shit," she let out in a whisper as the events of that morning came back to her: Cook, the space crawler, and the easy rider that knocked her off.

She glanced at the passenger seat – empty – then the back seat – empty.

She exhaled. That was not how she expected to conclude

the alien business, although there was still a chance to end up behind bars, unless she got out of there quickly.

Davis hadn't been kidding when tying the knot, hiding it behind the steering wheel and all. It took Lucy a while to work the straps, picking at them with the tip of her fingers, pausing occasionally when it felt like she was going to dislodge a bone or other. Eventually, she managed to loosen it enough to wriggle some manoeuvring space and get her hands free.

"That bitch," she murmured to herself, massaging her sore wrists. "Wait until I get my hands on her, and I'll show her."

She immediately turned on the engine and set the heaters to full blast to counteract the chill. An automatic gesture, half thinking about it. Only a moment later she realised the strangeness of it – pretend-badass Agent Davis had left her with the car keys.

Putting two and two together, she wasn't jumping to a conclusion so much as confidently striding towards it. Davis couldn't have been in her right mind when she left her there.

Still, she had to make sure. She got out into the rain to check the boot of the car. Empty. Unless the space crawler had gone hiding in the engine, there was little chance it was still around.

That felt too easy, though. No way had she kidnapped an alien from a secret laboratory, got caught, and let go again with a car as a goodbye gift.

Back in the driver's seat, rain dripping from her hair, Lucy stopped to think. She couldn't be sure she was out of danger. At least, she thought, she had been clever enough to take some intel away with her – or at least she thought she had.

The cup holder was empty of the plush sloth.

She slammed a hand on the steering wheel. "You've got to be kidding me!"

For a second, she contemplated giving it all up. The Skaara was probably on its journey of conquest already, while she could have just called Matthew, tell him the good news about the early release, and patch things up with a nice meal. They could forget the whole alien business, maybe lay low for a while, and she could get back to her life – whatever that meant.

She checked the time. She had been unconscious for almost two hours, and nobody had come to arrest her. That proved that at least she hadn't become the number one suspect for a potential alien invasion.

Maybe the space crawler still needed her. To hell with that.

She was still considering her options when her phone rang. She stared at Frank's name on the screen, until the phone registered the call as missed. He must have left the base, which meant the Skaara had at least honoured that part of the deal.

He had also probably heard about the alien's disappearance and figured out what had happened. Lucy could almost picture him riling up for a lecture – either that or he was tearing his hair out thinking she was being possessed. She could send him a text, reassure him she was still alive and well, and avoid his annoying reproach.

She got halfway through writing the message when the phone started ringing again. She closed her eyes and exhaled. He was just going to keep on calling, so might as well get it over with. Sliding her finger across the screen, she picked up the call.

"Please tell me the alien is not with you," he said before Lucy could utter a word.

"The alien is not with me," she replied.

"Is the alien telling you to say that?"

"Then why did you even ask me, genius?" Silence on the other end of the line. "Frankie, the alien is gone. That Agent

- VII -

Davis took it."

"What do you mean she took it? She wouldn't. I mean, she would, but what if that thing is doing to her what it did to me?"

"I wouldn't sweat it," she replied. "Even if that Skaara thing turned her evil, it's hardly our business. We're not the Avengers, you know? Let it go."

Frank's superhero complex, however, was running at full throttle. He wasn't going to let it go, so she suggested dinner instead.

After a quick Google search, they agreed to meet in a pub a few miles away. When she got there, maybe because of the gloomy weather, or maybe because of the low customer tide of a Thursday, an old shepherd dog was the only soul Lucy could see in the dim wooden light of the place. She had to call more than once before a blonde round woman appeared behind the counter. She didn't look too excited to be there either. After handing Lucy the menu, she stood waiting, tapping her fingers on the countertop, clearly eager to get away.

Two weeks of canteen food had had an impact on Lucy's appetite, and she found herself contemplating the scanty menu like a child gawping at his presents under the Christmas tree, wondering which one to pick first. She was about to ask for a burger and chips when Frank appeared by her side.

"We don't have time for food," he said, taking the menu out of her hands and giving it back to the bartender. "Two pints of lager and some peanuts, please."

Lucy was about to protest, then glanced at the woman, and something about her scowl made her think again. "What, they gave you pocket lunch on your way out?" she grumbled at her brother, while the pints were being poured.

"Maybe I just lost my appetite," he snapped back. "And yes,

97

they did offer me a sandwich."

He was mad, of course. What else was she expecting? "At least they let us out early," she attempted.

Frank only glared at her, as if he knew that it was her that made that possible. Better to let him stew for a minute before making more snarky comments.

When the not-so-jolly bartender placed the pints in front of them, Lucy grabbed both while Frank offered his card to the POS machine, which accepted the payment with a cheerful beep.

The woman was by then pouring as many as twelve peanuts in an espresso cup. She scowled at the machine first, then at Frank. They could have told her she had won the lottery, and she would have been just as excited.

At the back of the room, Lucy chose a corner table and sat down, turning her back to the wall and making sure she had a clear view of the entrance, in case an unwelcome somebody walked in. It was an old habit, but that day it felt particularly important.

"Do you want to tell me what the heck you were thinking?" asked Frank as he sat down and placed the cup of peanuts on the table.

"You know, it's generally unadvised to have alcohol on an empty stomach," she remarked, taking half of the peanuts for herself.

"Luce, be serious," he admonished, taking the rest of it.

"I'm very serious. Strongly unadvised."

Frank sat back and exhaled. Since the last time she saw him, he had grown thinner, and the black circle around his eyes had grown darker and deeper. "I just don't get it," he said.

"I don't expect you to."

"They would've let us out eventually, you know?"

She ignored his tone. "Fifty grand, dry-cleaning of my criminal record, and a free ticket out of puppet-land. Don't tell me you're not enjoying your freedom. And I'm not so sure they would've let us out eventually, to be honest."

"You unleashed a mind-controlling extra-terrestrial creature, which, incidentally, has got no money to give to anybody, nor the capacity to clean your criminal record," he shot back, leaning forward as he lowered his voice.

"Not the alien, genius," interjected Lucy. "The boss guy."

He frowned, spelling out his distrust one bit at a time. "The boss. As in Edward Cook, the Chief of Operations at SafeOp Defence Services. He's going to give you fifty thousand pounds."

"One day you'll regret your scepticism," she taunted him.

"Really? And when's that going to be? When I come visit you in jail, or when you'll be hiding from the police somewhere in Norway?"

That was uncalled for. Also, if she had to hide anywhere, she wasn't going to choose Norway. She shifted in her seat and took a sip of her lager. "Whatever."

"You shouldn't have done that, Luce." He leaned back, massaging his forehead. "And this free ticket out of puppet-land. Do you really believe that's a promise they're going to keep?"

Lucy could just about detect the patronising hint in his voice. She rested her elbows on the table and took a large sip of her beer, half wishing she could get drunk before having that conversation. "They will. I don't like being told what to do, you know that."

"Yeah, no kidding," he replied, then leaned forward across

the table one more time as he lowered his tone. "That's why I don't understand why you did it. You follow this alien's orders, and you call it freedom? You turned yourself into its minion, and the fact that you did it voluntarily doesn't change that. In fact, it makes it even worse."

They stared at each other long enough for Lucy to feel the dry air sting her eyes. He was right, but that was the only way to get both of them out of that creeper's influence.

After a few seconds, she took a swig of lager to mask her blinking. "I had no choice," she said finally. "They were going to force me to do it anyway. You know I'm right."

"Nice way of deflecting responsibility," he snapped back. "Jeez, Luce, we're not talking about stealing Mum's necklace here. Morality is not blurred. The distinction between right and wrong is as clear as blooming day."

"Your attempts at not swearing are adorable," she countered, doing her best to ignore the mention of their mother.

Looking down at the sticky table, she heard Frank exhale. When she looked up again, his beer was already down to half the pint, and he was intently rubbing the palm of his hand. Her confidence sank a bit lower. She had misjudged how disappointed he was going to be.

"So, what's next?" he asked. "Have you talked to Matt yet?"

"No, not yet. I was about to, when you called."

"What are you going to tell him?"

She shrugged. "We won the lottery for early release?"

"Are you going to stay with him tonight?"

"Why? Did *you* want to go stay with him?" she teased.

"Not unless you want me to tell him what happened."

No, she definitely didn't want that.

The silence extended until it became unbearable. Lucy's

fingers gripped the glass, as her leg started bouncing under the table. She had to say something to make it better, to show that she wasn't the horrible person he thought she was. "I think I know where the crawler is going next."

"You mean with Stephanie? Thank you very much, I already knew that."

She hadn't heard that tone since that one time he had to bail her out of prison. "You're on a first-name basis already? What, you're best friends now? She took the sloth from me, did you know that? I mean, that was petty."

Making Davis less of a good person felt like the only way she had not to sink any lower herself.

"Why would she take your ..." He stopped when he realised. "The flash drive. It's only a bunch of videos and songs. You'll get it back once we get out of this nightmare."

Only videos and songs and the whole lot of intel SafeOp's scientists had gathered on the Skaara menace. Lucy decided to keep that to herself for the time being. "We're already out of this nightmare, Frankie. What if we just go home and forget about this?"

"Forget about what?" he said with a snarl. "About the looming perspective of an alien invasion? Yeah, you go ahead and do that."

"It's not an invasion," she retorted. "The space crawler wanted me to take it places. Not Disneyland, though I asked, but one other specific place." She paused for effect. Frank didn't seem impressed. She sighed and rolled her eyes. "To its spaceship, Frankie. It's flying away."

He still didn't look convinced. "I doubt it wants to leave Earth already."

In fairness, Lucy wasn't convinced either.

"Even if that's true," he continued, "we should alert whoever is in charge at the landing site. They will know what to do."

"Or leave it be and let the space thing bugger off to where it came from."

"Luce, it's not leaving Earth, don't you get it? That thing came here for a reason, whatever that might be. We have to warn the authorities."

"Frankie, that's not going to work!"

He recoiled at her impetus.

She settled back down and tried to explain. "Davis is not the only one who's not in her right mind. I told you, it's Cook who's orchestrating all this, and he's got an alien brain of his own. How do you think I made it out of that place?"

It took Frank a moment to take it all in. "You weren't joking."

"Of course I wasn't joking, you idiot. What kind of weirdo do you think I am, making up stuff like that?" She realised she had raised her voice, so she quieted down to continue. "He kicked Davis out of the room and turned off the cameras. I thought he was going to pull some bad-cop trick on me. Instead, he asked me to pull off the heist of the galaxy. I'm paraphrasing here, but you get the point."

She watched Frank clench his jaw, and she recognised the expression on his face. He was finally getting it. They sipped their beers in silence.

"We have to find it," started Frank, dropping his hand on the table.

Lucy jumped in her seat, then stared at him for a second. "That is the stupidest thing I've ever heard you say. Why would you go chasing the same space crawler that already hijacked your brain once? What's wrong with you?"

"That thing is planning something. What if we are the only

two people who know? The only ones who can stop it?"

"Hold on." Lucy held her hands up to stop what would soon become a suicidal rambling. "First, you've got to remember we are nobodies. Even if we made it to the landing site, we're civilians – they'll think we're nutters. Second, there is really nothing telling us that that poor thing doesn't just want to get into its spaceship and go home, and third..." She held her hands higher to prevent Frank from opposing her second point. They both knew the Skaara wasn't just going to fly away. "Third, let's say we find the space crawler. What do you suggest doing then? Sweet talk it into crawling back into its cage?"

Frank blinked at her.

She relaxed back on the chair. "You hadn't thought about it."

Her phone pinged in her pocket. She did her best to ignore it, while her brother didn't seem to notice. He was staring intently at the rest of his lager, as if the beer was going to give him the answers he needed.

Lucy slid the phone out of her pocket and activated the screen, glancing down at the sender of the message.

"There's got to be a way," said Frank, pulling her attention back to the conversation. He looked hopeless. "Matt's parents have connections pretty much everywhere; maybe they can help."

"We are not bringing Matt into this."

"Luce, he's going to find out eventually."

"We are not, and that's not up for debate."

They sat like that for a moment longer. There was still something that was nagging at Lucy.

"How did you know she came after me?"

He raised an eyebrow at her. "You mean aside from the whole base being on high alert? Everyone was talking about it when I

103

left."

"How do you know she didn't get back?"

He hesitated. "Well, you're here. How did you know that thing is with Stephanie?"

"Alien gone, keys in the ignition, me not arrested," she dismissed quickly. "How did she know to come after me?"

Frank looked at her as if he had been pinched. "Are you serious? I see you for the first time since we got there, and you start telling me about the friends you've made, and how they're letting us out early, and what little you care about whatever happens to that thing we found in the woods. Guess what? It sounded suspicious as ..." He hesitated on the word.

Lucy smirked at him. "You can say *fuck*," she encouraged him.

"Well, yes. It was suspicious as *fuck*," he concluded, lowering his voice.

"Well, joke's on you, because now the crawler from outer space is riding a fully-trained killing machine."

"Stephanie is not a killing machine," he replied.

Lucy grimaced. "You really have to stop calling her by her first name. It's weird."

"No, it's not," he replied defensively, then pursed his lips, "What happened when she caught up with you?"

"She knocked me unconscious and tied me to the steering wheel," she replied. "Oh, and she stole the sloth."

"And here I thought you two could be great friends," he mocked her. "Do you have any idea what happened next?"

Lucy gave him a dull stare. "No, sorry, I forgot to astral project while she was choke holding me."

He downed the rest of his beer. "At least she didn't shoot you."

She couldn't figure out if he was joking. "She bloody well tried!"

He kept a straight face for the whole of two seconds, before erupting in laughter. The old shepherd dog turned to check what the fun was, then went back to sleep, unimpressed. "Oh, come on, you can't believe she would have!"

Lucy didn't feel like joining in the laughter. Being held at gunpoint was very low on her list of fun things to do. She drank the rest of her beer, then stood up from the table, eager to get away from the rest of the conversation.

Frank called after her, "Where are you going?"

"To find the space crawler," she said. "Or have you changed your mind while being hilarious over there?"

He cleared his throat, catching up on the change of atmosphere. He stood up and joined her on the way out. "You changed your mind?"

"Evidently. I'm not letting you go after that thing on your own, so I might as well make sure you don't do anything stupid."

"Why does it sound like you have a plan?"

Not a plan; a text message. "Davis either went straight to the landing site, or she went home," she explained. As she unlocked the phone, she cleared the notification for the unread message and opened the online map. "It can't be that hard to find out where she lives. As you said, Matt's family has connections."

"Have you also figured out what we're going to do when we find it?"

"*We* are not going to find anything," she rebuked him. "*I'll* go after Davis, and maybe lock her in a room somewhere, until the cavalry comes in."

Her brother was suddenly in front of her, blocking her way.

"Luce, that's not a good idea. She knocked you out and tied you to the steering wheel of the car not three hours ago," he said, attracting an impressed glance from the bartender.

"I know. I was there." She pushed past him and out the door into the car park. She gazed around her in the cold, damp November air. She heard the door of the pub close behind her, then Frank's steps on the gravel.

"Well, then maybe I should go."

"You've got to manage your crush on the secret agent," she teased.

"Stop it."

Lucy exhaled, then turned to face him. "The crawler got you once. I'm not going to let it get to you again. End of story."

Frank opened his mouth to reply, then closed it. He conceded. "Fine. How are you going to find out where she lives without telling Matt what happened?"

"I have my ways," she said. "Where's your car?"

"Left it a mile down that way," he said, gesturing towards a bend in the road.

She waved towards the red Corsa she had left in the pub's car park. "I'm right here."

"You couldn't have gotten something flashier, since you're only driving it without a licence," he remarked.

"Not my choice," she told him. "Listen, I'll call you tomorrow. Just don't do anything stupid until you hear from me, okay?"

"Hold on. No, you call me when you get there. If Stephanie has that thing, it's just as dangerous for you as it would be for me."

"The crawler trusts me, Frankie. I got it out, remember? It's going to be okay."

"Just be sensible, Luce," he said, but she was already walking away.

"Go home, Frankie." She raised a hand as a sort of backward wave and walked to the flashy car. She had to get rid of it as soon as possible.

Once sitting inside, she checked the text message on her phone. It was from Cook. A lonely alien in a foreign world was going to need all the help it could get. It was a bit annoying that it couldn't do it without threatening her brother in the same sentence.

You and your brother are still not out of it, he had written, followed by an address in Filton, north of Bristol.

She typed her reply and hit send, then turned the keys in the ignition.

- VIII -

Stephanie stood next to the motorcycle, daylight dimming into twilight. She couldn't remember how she got there. She didn't even remember getting off the bike, nor taking the helmet off. She had been locked in a dark room — the boot of the metaphorical car that was her mind — for who knew how long.

She remembered the Chief moving aside to give her a clear view of the backpack — or maybe to give the Skaara a clear view of her. Then the bag had moved. Then the gunshot.

She had no memory of seeing the creature, even as it jumped out at her, yet she felt it scratching her back as it hung onto her shirt. Oddly enough, it was the only thing she could feel.

Her skin didn't register the crispy evening temperature, and she was aware of a hole in her stomach after an entire day gone without eating. Yet she didn't feel hungry, per se.

At least, she thought, she was finally conscious, and that was an improvement. Remembering Frank's experience of the Skaara's control, she wondered if her sudden consciousness meant there was a chance for her to fight back, or if she had just been given the privilege of a window view instead of being trapped in the boot.

One thing she knew: there wasn't any rescue coming for her. The Chief's behaviour had been clear enough.

Across the road, a man walked his dog past her apartment block, and the lamplight above the door turned its faded light on them, even though darkness was still a little while to come. The hound stopped and turned to look at Stephanie, baring his teeth in a growl.

Good doggy, she thought. *Come and get the space invader*. Then the owner pulled him along and soon both disappeared around the corner.

She couldn't understand why the Skaara had taken her back home – not until she did. As if something had placed the thought inside her brain, she knew the alien was tired. A whole day of escaping and controlling had been exhausting. It needed a safe place to rest.

No. Stephanie forced that train of thought to stop. She was never going to give that creature a safe harbour, especially not in her home. Years of therapy had taught her to battle her demons. This one was just a bit more corporeal than most.

She made a motion to turn around and get back on the motorcycle – or at least she was sure she had instructed her body to do that. The apartment block stubbornly remained in front of her. She remembered reading about how the human brain could be tricked by perception, how people thought they were moving their limbs even after they had lost them. Stephanie now thought she understood how that felt, as she tried to move a body that wasn't hers to move anymore.

She only knew she had started walking when the world began shifting around her and the apartment building started getting closer. She was crossing the street. There was a feeling of nausea, right before she realised there wasn't an actual body to throw up anything with. She tried to tune herself into the movement, ease the dizziness. It wasn't much different than sitting on a still train while the carriage beside her moved along.

The light above the front door flickered off for a moment, then the motion sensor detected her and turned the lamplight on again.

When she finally stood in front of the door, a thought popped into her head, like a viscous inner voice wondering where she had put her keys. In the right pocket of her jacket as usual, she thought automatically, and as soon as she did, her right hand moved up to find the pocket and the keys.

While her hands worked through the keys to find the right one, Stephanie watched her thoughts. She understood what just happened. The Skaara had asked her a question, and she had promptly responded.

Maybe the alien wasn't as all-powerful on a person's mind as she had expected. Maybe it couldn't absorb all of a human's knowledge as easily as tapping water from a wellspring.

As soon as the Skaara had her stepping through the door, Mrs Widdicombe made her appearance in the hallway. She was the building administrator and major thorn in everybody's side. Interactions with her required all of Stephanie's mindful presence on a good day.

"Look who the cat dragged in," the old woman said, arms akimbo, her words filled to the brim with bitter sarcasm. "Three days I've spent waiting to catch you. Three days!" She held up three fingers to show the inhumane amount of time Stephanie had spent avoiding her.

It was the typical welcome home. The correct response, which Stephanie had perfected over the years, would have been to ignore the old woman's tone and wish her a good evening. The Skaara, however, wasn't picking up the suggestion.

"Mrs Widdicombe," she heard herself saying, "what seems

to be the matter?"

That was completely out of character, and the old crone was just as perplexed. Nonetheless, she quickly resumed her rant. "I should think you believe this building looks after itself. I had to take out the bins myself yesterday. Again. At my age!"

There was a moment of silence, as if the Skaara didn't know how to reply to something that wasn't a question, so Mrs Widdicombe charged on. "And do you think this is a post office dump, where you can leave your mail all over the place? You clean that up, or I'll throw it out with the rubbish, do you hear me?"

That was a bit overdramatic, but the old woman was in full swing, and there was no discomfort too minor to be mentioned. Stephanie had experienced the treatment often enough to know that.

"Work duty has kept me away," the Skaara finally managed, "I'll take my mail."

When she turned, however, amongst all the mail received and stacked on the shelf, there wasn't anything addressed to Stephanie Davis. Before she could formulate any coherent solution and present it to the alien mastermind, she saw her own hand pick up one of the flyers. Stephanie wondered if the Skaara had any understanding of earthlings' mail system.

Mrs Widdicombe was just as doubtful. "Are those pizza coupons?"

None of the two minds behind Stephanie's mouth could come up with a credible response for that. Before she could utter a word, a thick voice bellowed from the top of the stairs. "Leave the lovely lady."

Swooping in superhero style, a compact young man toddled down the stairs. For the first time since she met him, Stephanie was grateful to see him.

In the privacy of her mind, she thought of him as Casanova. Not because of his heritage, and certainly not because of his success with women, but because of his confidence and persistence in showcasing both. His actual name was Dennis, born of Italian parents in a small town near Woking, and raised to be the hero to any damsel – in distress or not – he found along the way. No doubt he called it chivalry.

The Skaara hanging on Stephanie's back was less than grateful for the extra witness. "It's okay. You don't need to –"

Casanova, however, was on a roll. "I know, I know. You are a strong woman," he interjected, "but I take care."

After thirty years in England, he still considered English grammar an unnecessary nuisance. It was a mystery to everyone how he had made it through school at all.

"Take care of what?" jolted Mrs Widdicombe. "The bins went out yesterday, and yours too, mister. I took them out. You took care of nothing, as usual."

The man hesitated, confused by the response. His hand went to the hem of his T-shirt as he started playing with the fabric, much like a child would when caught.

Stephanie would have felt sorry for him if it hadn't been for his over-the-top machismo. She allowed herself a snigger. Watching the scene unfold was a bit like standing backstage at a lifelike play. Not that she was enjoying the Skaara's control, but she was starting to see the silver lining.

While Mrs Widdicombe kept her discontent aimed at Casanova, firing at him the extensive evidence of his negligence and slackness, Stephanie noticed a noise coming from the floor above. In a moment, the crew was going to be complete.

Beary Bob, real name Bob Colton, was the only tenant

Stephanie could call her friend – not only because he didn't stalk her down the stairs like the other two, but because he was a genuinely good person. She would know. She had done a thorough check on him.

"Steph, you're back," he bellowed from the top of the stairs, breaking up Mrs Widdicombe's tirade. "I wanted to show you something. Could you come up a second?"

That was her way out. Stephanie pushed with all her will to get the Skaara to understand that. *Move*, she thought. *Follow him, please.*

The creature must have been open to suggestions. "Sure," she heard herself saying. Then the world started shifting once again, and she was moving.

As she brushed past Casanova on her way up the stairs, he turned his attention away from Mrs Widdicombe to wink at her and whisper, "Hey, beautiful."

Stephanie cringed slightly, relieved to see that at least he wasn't making any attempt at touching her – he had done that once and lived to regret it. She couldn't be sure the Skaara would be so lenient.

Past the next flight of stairs, Bob was standing at his door, waiting for her. "How are you doing, Steph?"

"I'm doing okay, thanks. How are you doing?" she replied – human conversation 101. The Skaara was again in full control.

"Awesome," he replied with a big grin on his face. "Steve's cousin came by. I told him you'd be away until next week."

"That's great, thank you," offered the alien. A flat comment to Bob's efforts at keeping Stephanie's admirer out of the way. She made a note to invite him over for film night soon, if she ever got out of that alien mess.

Bob lingered at the door. Stephanie lingered too. It was time to go, yet the alien didn't seem to have gotten the memo. It was a full couple of awkward seconds before she finally heard her voice saying, "I have to go. Thanks for the save."

"Anytime." He looked perplexed, yet he still smiled through his beard before disappearing inside, while Stephanie continued up the stairs to the second floor.

This time, her hands found the keys without hesitation, and the door opened noiselessly into her one-bedroom flat. She stepped inside and closed the door securely behind her, yet something made her wonder if that was indeed a safe place for her to be. She brushed the thought away. Those weren't her doubts, but the Skaara's.

She unclipped her gun and placed it on the coffee table, together with her phone. The creature was making her lay down her weapons, getting ready to leave its host. Clever.

As the Skaara crawled off her back, Stephanie felt herself sliding into her own bones and muscles again. If until then she had been peeking at the world from behind the curtain, now she was stepping onto the stage. The world was all around her once again. It was exhilarating, until the pain came knocking.

A sharp, burning pain lingered just below her shoulder blades. She caught her breath, then exhaled through it. However bad that was, it had to wait.

The creature scuttled across the floor of the living room, then climbed onto the sofa to curl up on the seat closest to the coffee table. A snake body with snake arms – or tentacles, she considered. One of its extremities – possibly its head, if there was a head at all – was perked up, standing guard.

Stephanie was still holding the keys. She ran her thumb along the jagged edge, up to the dull tip. Pointless. She shook the thought out of her head. Even if she had been able to get close enough to jab the key into the alien's body, the chances of a mortal blow were scant, while those of her getting back under its control were through the roof.

She left the keys in her pocket and took off the jacket and dropped it across the armrest of the sofa. Whatever way the Skaara had been hanging on to her, it had drawn blood. She could feel her shirt sticking to her skin as she moved her arms about.

The creature didn't seem to notice she was leaving the room – or at least didn't care.

In her bedroom, she took off her top and stood in front of the mirror, twisting around to see a couple of purple rashes just underneath the shoulder blades, both dotted with red droplets. She took a deep breath, and the skin strained against the straps of her bra.

"I'd appreciate it if you left my back alone next time you hitch a ride," she called to the other room – as if the Skaara could hear and understand.

She took off her bra and let the skin breathe for a moment before figuring out how to take care of those wounds on her own.

There had to be a way out of that creature's control. If she could understand how it worked, maybe she could have tried something to at least dazzle it and give her time to lock it up somewhere safe, until the good guys came to collect. She remembered something the science team had mentioned about benzodiazepines, and she almost regretted turning down a Xanax prescription when the therapist had offered one.

Another option was to make a run for the door and lock the Skaara inside. The cost of a failed attempt, however, was likely to be higher than she could afford – she still had no memory of the ride home, and she couldn't remember what happened to the motorcycle helmet.

Then there was Lucy Campbell. Someone had tasked her with stealing the alien creature, and the girl had somehow persuaded the Skaara to leave her alone. The creature had sat in the passenger seat, safely at arm's length. If Stephanie could find a way to do the same for herself, she could maybe manage to keep control of her body, even with the Skaara around her keeping guard.

Not ideal, but at least it gave her an option. Between killing the wretched thing and facilitating a planetary invasion, there had to be room for compromise.

Lucy Campbell. Something kept on nagging her about the girl. The way she hinted at the backpack was so deliberate, as if she wanted to tell her something. She had offered the Skaara to her, even if it had sounded like a jest. It was just possible she had actually been serious.

With the pain finally subsiding, she went to the bathroom cabinet and soaked some gauze in hydroperoxide, which she then applied to the reddened skin that she could reach. She gripped the sink as the searing pain burnt through her. Part of her even welcomed the overwhelming sensation.

As she was wiping away the last of the bloody droplets, wincing at each touch, someone knocked at the door. *Not a great time for visitors*, she thought. She considered ignoring them until they went away.

She took her time to go to the closet and take out a clean shirt, paying extra care not to brush the fabric against the sore skin as she put it on. Just as slowly, she made her way out of the bedroom and into the living room. Every movement seemed to stretch the skin on her back into a painful sting.

Whoever was at the door knocked again, and Stephanie saw the Skaara stir and perk up. The last thing she wanted was to alarm the alien and end up in a mental blackout once again.

"It's okay, I got this," she said, hoping to be left alone to deal with the visitor.

She made it all the way to the door before something pinned her leg. The world went blurry for a second, before she found herself standing backstage once more.

- IX -

The old lady was still watching Lucy from the bottom of the stairs, craning her neck in a way that could hardly have been comfortable. She could feel her judgmental stare drilling a whole into the side of her skull.

When Lucy knocked again, the woman bent a bit further. She was like a watchdog, tracking suspicious faces hanging around the hall. She was doing an excellent job, Lucy had to admit.

"Don't worry about her, she's all smoke and no bite," said the upstairs tenant. Lucy frowned, fighting the impulse to correct that weirdly mixed-up saying.

Much friendlier than the old lady, that cheap version of Don Jon had swooped in to introduce himself and offer his assistance in finding Davis. Yes, she lived there. Yes, she was home. And would Lucy want to join him for a glass of wine – but no, Lucy wouldn't want that. No, not even for a gorgeous Trebbiano delle Puglie, whatever that was.

He had been on his way back up to his own apartment for a while already, taking the steps backwards for a chance to keep the conversation going. She entertained the idea of tripping him and making it look like an accident. Nothing that would injure him permanently, just enough for a mild concussion.

"You know," he persevered, oblivious of the risk he was

taking, "if Steph don't open, I can cook dinner for you instead."
He lingered by the handrail, waiting for her to fall at his feet.
"I make pasta for you."

At the mention of food, Lucy's stomach growled. If the
creep had food to offer, maybe it would be worth giving him
a chance. Maybe, *if Steph don't open*. She sized him up – she
could probably take him if he got too handsy.

She wondered what was taking Davis so long, if something
had gone wrong with the space crawler. Maybe she had tried
to fight back, and the little bugger had turned her brain into
mush in retaliation. If that was the case, having dinner with a
plus-size Don Jon was definitely a better option for the evening.

She was about to say something when the door finally opened.
Davis looked at her, then up towards the stocky Italian man. He
waved at them, sporting his own version of a smouldering look,
then lingered a bit more, until Lucy finally stepped through the
door.

Looking at Davis, something was off. Not *off* as in *wrong*
– although there was a lot of that too – but more like *off* as
in *turned off*. Davis' gaze was dull, absent. Her movements
looked like an afterthought, so different from the controlled
determination she had displayed when they had first met. Lucy
had thought about the idea of her brain turning into mush as
an evocative figure of speech, but she was starting to believe
that it could be an accurate description of the alien's effect on
people. If that was true, her brother got away lightly.

Inside the apartment, she looked around the open-plan living
room, clocking the door to the bedroom and the one to the
bathroom. No sign of the space crawler anywhere, which
confirmed Lucy's suspicions.

As sorry as she felt for Davis, it was reassuring to know that the space crawler was going to leave her alone, as long as it had to keep its tentacle on the killing machine.

She heard the door close behind her. "I hope your dinner options are better than pasta," she said as she moved to the kitchen island. "I have trouble sleeping when I eat carbs in the evening."

She ran her fingers along the ridge of one of the stools.

"You can sit," offered Davis. She was still standing by the door.

"That goes for you too," replied Lucy.

After a quick glance at the stools, Davis walked past them and to the fridge. "Can I offer you a drink?" she said, her hand resting on the door handle.

"I can eat if you have some food," Lucy countered taking off her jacket and laying it on one of the seats.

Davis stood idle for a moment, then went to the cupboard and produced a pack of cream crackers. "My pleasure."

Lucy cocked her head at that stunted display. "Are you browsing through human hospitality rules, or are you genuinely trying to be nice?"

Settling on one of the stools, Lucy started on the crackers, before either human or alien could decide to take them away. Her stomach grumbled in pleasure as she nibbled away. Two crackers later, Davis was still idling on the spot, like a video-game character waiting for input.

Talking to empty shells of people was getting on Lucy's nerves, even more so when the wretched space crawler insisted on keeping up that pretence at human conversation. "Why don't you let me speak with her?" she suggested. "We could show you how it's done."

"I don't trust this one," said the alien behind Davis' eyes.

120

"I can handle her," replied Lucy. The Skaara didn't reply but didn't relinquish control either. Lucy rolled her eyes. "Suit yourself."

There was a short silence, one more cracker was eaten, then she exhaled. "Does she have beer?"

It was a moment before Davis replied, "Beer is alcohol."

"Which is what I need to get through this thing we're doing. If there's no beer, vodka is fine too." She reached out a hand, hoping that would end the conversation.

Alas, it wasn't meant to be. "Alcohol is poison. I can't allow it."

Lucy felt a sting of disappointment, yet the reward was worth it. She tucked away the information and went back to nibbling on her crackers. "Well, I guess we'll just have to remember that for next time."

She held eye contact, wondering if Davis was watching them, maybe even taking notes, while being locked away at the back of her mind – if she was even conscious at all.

"Why are you here?" the Skaara asked.

"I was hoping you would tell me that. Your sidekick brain told me to come find you, gave me the address and all."

"You're worried about your brother."

You bet I am, thought Lucy. "He can turn potatoes into vodka. I have reasons to keep his brain intact. Also, the deal was for a free pass out of mush-brain land if I helped you. That's quite appealing too. I'm sure Davis here would agree with me. Besides, you stole my pink sloth, and I want it back."

Davis – or the Skaara – recoiled. Lucy wasn't quite sure if that was due to the mention of alcohol, or the sloth. She decided both would work fine. "It's a keyring, pink and fuzzy, and looks like a sloth. Totally harmless. She stole it when she knocked me out, I suppose. Do you mind if I get it back?"

In Davis' dull stare, Lucy pictured the space crawler rummaging through piles of boxes of information stored in the woman's brain, while what was left of the human frantically threw them out of a metaphorical mind window. Frank probably would've found tons of things wrong with that metaphor, but Lucy quite enjoyed the image and barely held back a smile at the thought.

Finally, the Skaara conceded. "The left pocket of her jacket."

Not enough of an answer. She asked again, "Do you mind if I take it back?"

"What's so important about it?"

"My brother gave it to me a long time ago. It's a bunch of photos and birthday videos. It's only sentimental importance."

Davis probably hadn't had a chance to examine the flash drive, and the space crawler couldn't have realised what she had been downloading in the lab – not from inside the cage, not from that distance. With some luck, Lucy was the only one in the room who knew what that sloth really meant.

After some thought, Davis nodded almost imperceptibly.

The jacket had been thrown on the sofa's armrest. It was one of those waterproof hooded jackets with more pockets than fashion sense. Inside the left pocket, Lucy's fingers wrapped around something furry. She pulled out the sloth, held it up victoriously, then went back to her stool and shoved it in the pocket of her own jacket – the same waterproof hooded nonsense that Matthew had made her wear for their walk in the woods. The realisation made her almost self-conscious.

She glanced at the door, only a few feet away. She had taken the flash drive back; she could have run out and closed the door between her and the space crawler before the little thing could even realise what was happening. She could have called the police, or the army, and passed the flash drive on to them. She could have gotten away from all that nonsense.

As if, she thought. Davis was probably going to throw a knife at her if she tried. Hopefulness was such a foolish business.

She sat back on the stool. "What is it you need me for, then?"

"Do you have means of transport?"

"I have the flashy red car Cook gave me to get you out."

Davis shook her head. "That vehicle is connected to my escape. You'll need to find another way."

"If anybody had been looking for it, I wouldn't be here telling you about it," she pointed out. "The car was left two miles from the base for almost two hours, with me sleeping in it, and nobody even came knocking at the window. We're fine."

As if she was reading some very tiny print, Davis squinted into the distance. "The army is now involved, and a search party was sent out looking for you and the car. Edward delayed them as much as he could, but you have to find another way."

It was only through context that Lucy figured out she was talking about Cook. "Wait, are you doing the thing now? Are you talking to Cook via the remote-control nugget of brain? You know, I kind of wish I had that in high school. Before I dropped off, that is." She didn't, but it seemed like a good way to mark how terrifying the idea of the nugget brain was.

"The car is not safe. Find another way."

Whatever, thought Lucy. She had no idea how to get another car, other than stealing it, which would defeat the whole purpose. "Since I'd rather not go around breaking into cars, maybe someone can drive me?"

A few seconds passed, and Davis only gave her a dull stare in response.

"Fine," said Lucy, taking that as a yes. "I'll get somebody to drive me, then. Give me just a second."

She hadn't even unlocked the screen of her phone when Davis sprang across the kitchen isle to snatch it away. Lucy held on to it, panic flexing her fingers around the device. Her eyes were fixed on the woman's face, and she was sure she could see panic in her expression too.

Static sizzled in the air around them. Their grips were tight in the frozen moment.

There was a real chance the Skaara was about to move from Davis onto her. Lucy wasn't sure what that would mean for Davis, but she definitely didn't like what it would mean for herself. She didn't dare look down at her hand, in fear of seeing a tentacle coming out of Davis' sleeve.

"Let go of my phone," Lucy said slowly.

There was no visible reaction to that. Lucy thought about letting go herself, but hell if she was going to let that thing take her phone.

She slowly lifted her free hand and laid it on Davis'. She half expected to touch the Skaara's skin. Instead, it was all human, and it looked like Davis felt it too. For a moment, her eyes almost recovered a glint of humanity, as if she had managed to draw the curtains open, and she was waving at Lucy from behind the glass. Then it all glazed over again, and her hold on the phone softened, until she finally pulled away.

Lucy took a second to remember how to breathe, before going back to her phone. She cleared her throat.

"Who are you contacting?" asked Davis.

"Matthew Cavell," she said before she could stop herself.

"Who is he to you?"

Lucy took her eyes briefly off the screen of her smartphone. "He's the most harmless human being you can find, and he does have a car." She checked her tone, trying not to antagonise the space crawler too much. "He's useful, that's what Matt is. Why? Who is he to you?"

"A human being," replied the Skaara. The same tone could have been used to call him *alien-killer*.

Lucy raised an eyebrow at that. The idea of Matthew being a threat to anyone was simply ridiculous. "Well, unless Mattie is public enemy number two in your books, he's going to be the human being I'll be riding with."

"You trust him with the mission?"

"You mean your mission?" she asked, then snorted. "I trust he won't understand there even is a mission."

Davis nodded, then walked to a cupboard in the living room, where she busied herself looking for something. She walked back to the kitchen corner a moment later, holding pen and paper.

"Seriously? What is this, 1995? Can't you, like, send me the location on the phone or something? It worked fine to get me here. I'm sure it'll work again."

Her comment went ignored, while Davis' hands scribbled a time and an address, then folded the piece of paper and handed it over. "There is a second retrieval that you'll be required to do. Edward will send you the details in a text message."

"Right, so Cook is the tech savvy of the lot. I have to say, I'm starting to wonder how you guys even managed space travel."

"Is this Matthew able to drive you to a place called Partridge Manor?"

Lucy knew that place. Matthew's parents had a place in the countryside called Partridge. She could not remember if it was a manor, but there couldn't be many Partridge-named places around, surely.

125

She nodded to Davis, hoping neither she nor the alien had spotted her reaction.

It looked like they hadn't. Davis waved towards the door. "You can leave now. Don't be late."

- X -

It hadn't been a restful night for Stephanie. The rashes on her back hadn't given her peace, itching at the edges and stinging when the bedsheets brushed against them.

While sleep eluded her, the conversation with Lucy kept on replaying in her head – her confidence in talking to the Skaara, her touch before she pulled her hand away, and her reaction when Partridge Manor was mentioned. She was planning something, and that pink sloth had everything to do with that.

Around 5 a.m. Stephanie finally gave up trying to sleep. It felt as if she had barely closed her eyes. She was exhausted, almost longing for the Skaara to take over if that meant that she could tuck herself away and rest a bit longer.

The warm shower helped her wake up a little more, although it was a complicated matter to keep the scratches on her back clear of the flowing water. The pain, however, turned out to be deceiving. As she checked herself in the mirror, it was much better than she had expected. She stuck a large enough plaster on the wounds, then picked a sports bra and a black top from the wardrobe.

What was worse than she had hoped was her face. Dark circles under her eyes betrayed her dramatically low energy levels. She combed her hair and pulled it up in a ponytail. It didn't look any better, so she let it drop back on her shoulders and brushed it a bit more. The elastic band, she kept around her wrist.

Walking to the kitchen, she stole a glance at the alien creature nested in the corner of the sofa. She was sure it was awake. The Skaara. It had left her alone all night. Maybe it had been a test. Or maybe it just needed a night of rest before the long day ahead.

The fridge was alarmingly empty. She boiled a couple of eggs and grabbed a protein bar from the cupboard. After being neglected for days, the orange juice didn't smell right, so she opted for a glass of water instead. As for coffee, there wasn't any.

Thinking back to Lucy's beer request and the Skaara's stark response, Stephanie almost wished she had a beer to use as a breakfast treat.

"Would you mind if we stopped for coffee on the way?" she asked out loud, checking the alien's reaction.

The Skaara stirred. She gulped her iron pills with the water.

As she chewed on the protein bar, her thoughts went to the address she had herself written down and given Lucy. She knew where it was, the same way she had known to write it down – the Skaara knew. More puzzling was what the creature hoped to get from a furniture shop. It was unlikely to be for spaceship redecoration purposes.

The Skaara had barely moved since she had walked into the room. If the creature was indeed still asleep, maybe she could make it out of the flat and lock the wretched thing inside, call the army, catch the Chief red-handed, and get it all over with.

She eyed the jacket still lying on the sofa – that was clearly not an option. Her phone as well had to stay behind, together with the gun. Not a problem. She could figure out something else. Maybe ask Beary Bob to lend her his phone.

She counted the steps to the door and planned her move. There was little to no margin for error, but Stephanie knew she could do it.

Throwing away the wrapper of the protein bar, she managed to get two steps closer to the door without raising suspicion, then she sprinted.

She just about managed to get to the door before something pushed her back. Reality grew thinner around her, and once again she was sitting backstage.

The Skaara hadn't been sleeping after all.

Her body stood still for a second, then she walked back a few steps, and her arm went to grab her jacket and put it on before picking up the gun. The phone stayed where it was.

As early in the morning as it was – the clock had just struck six – nobody bothered her on the way down and out of the building. The helmet turned out to have been secured to the motorbike, while the key was in the small breast pocket of the jacket. As for driving it, it looked like the Skaara had worked out the vehicle on its own.

As they left the neighbourhood behind them, Stephanie allowed her mind to drift. The lack of sleep and the steady hum of the engine combined to lull her into a light doze. Her thoughts kept on going back to Lucy and the address she had scribbled for her.

She remembered something the girl had said. The mention of a sidekick brain. The Chief was conspiring with the Skaara, that much she had already figured out. Lucy's comment suggested it was more than a simple cooperation. The implications of that were horrifying.

On top of all that was the reference to Partridge Manor. The name had been enough to remind her where she had heard the name of Mr Cavell before. He was the husband of Lady Eliza Jane Cavell, née Partridge, and current resident of the Partridge Estate in the Highlands, the same place metres away from the beacon that had been actioned two days prior the spaceship being discovered.

The Skaara had picked its servants well.

The oddest piece of the puzzle was that fuzzy keyring. Stephanie knew about the flash drive inside, yet it looked like Lucy was trying to keep that a secret. Something told her it had more than sentimental value. If the alien was still threatening her or Frank, maybe the flash drive contained something she could use as leverage.

While Stephanie was lost in her train of thought, the scene around her had started to change, houses quickly replaced with fir and oak trees. The motorbike slowed down considerably as they turned into the woods, tyres sliding on the muddy track the army had created amongst the trees.

As they approached the landing site, it looked increasingly like a secret base in a foreign land.

The Skaara decided it was better to leave the motorcycle outside by the security entrance. After removing her helmet, Stephanie approached the gate.

The army takeover had been a small mercy. As much damage as the Chief might have done already, at least he and the Skaara didn't have complete control over the site anymore.

The soldier at the guard post asked for her name and badge, noted that she was carrying a firearm, before they finally let her go wishing her a good day.

Past security, Stephanie was met with a multitude of marquees nested amongst the trees – even SafeOp's sponsors couldn't get permission to knock down a full acre of National Reserve to make space for an improvised base camp, not even if it was because of an extra-terrestrial spaceship.

With the Skaara running her body full steam ahead, Stephanie felt her grip on the world slip away, the edges getting blurry, a hint of nausea she didn't quite know where to place.

The base was a buzzing hive of activity. As both soldiers and SafeOp agents walked past, her head turning one way and the other, Stephanie had to stop looking and let the body take care of itself. The Skaara had tightened its control so much that her being conscious or not made no difference. It made her wonder why it was keeping her conscious at all.

When she opened her eyes, her body had finally stopped moving.

Outside one of the marquees, the Chief was waiting for them, holding a take-away cup in each hand. Even in that detached state, Stephanie felt the anticipation gripping her – she couldn't get her hands on that coffee quick enough. The Skaara, however, was resisting the impulse.

"Glad to see you made it through unscathed," he said by way of greeting once they were close enough. He was talking to the Skaara as if Stephanie wasn't even there.

"You seem surprised," replied Stephanie's voice. There was something rightfully threatening about the tone.

"I'm more surprised that everybody else is," he replied, a wide grin on his face. He finally handed over one of the coffees. "Here. Davis will be grateful."

Please take it, begged Stephanie in her head. Then her hand reached forward and grabbed the mug. She took a sip, and even the vicarious taste of sweet coffee made her cringe. "It's disgusting," she heard herself saying. "I don't think Davis likes it either."

"I suppose I shouldn't have let Victoria take care of it," the Chief replied.

It was settled, then. Victoria Evans had been promoted to Skaara's PA. Not an impressive choice, but still one more thing she had to worry about. For once, Stephanie wasn't finding it hard to believe that Evans was helping of her own free will – she had probably volunteered, if anything.

The Chief gestured towards the marquee behind him. "Our first stop will be the observation room."

"The vehicle is priority."

"The vehicle is under surveillance."

Stephanie held back a breath of relief. The army was going to figure out they were tampering with the surveillance system. For once, the Chief had bitten off more than he could chew, unless the limits of what he could achieve had moved that much further ahead.

Inside the marquee, ten different screens showed ten different angles of the spaceship and of the hangar that had been built around it. Three soldiers were monitoring the images, occasionally zooming in on any speck of dust that looked too excited to be there.

A slender moustachioed man stood up to greet them. "Edward Cook, as I live and breathe," he said, offering a hand that the Chief shook enthusiastically with both of his.

"Sergeant Marker, it's an absolute pleasure to see you."

"Yeah right, as if you were happy that we took over," remarked the sergeant. "I didn't think I'd see you around here, after you got that warning."

"Some friends put in a good word for me," the Chief replied. His flat tone could have sounded cold to people who didn't know it was an alien creature speaking through him.

The other three soldiers in the room had turned to look at them. The sergeant wasn't going to bring them in the loop, though. "Boys, thanks for your hard work, but I have to ask you to leave. It's a highly sensitive matter that Edward and I have to discuss."

The soldiers exchanged a look, then the one sitting in the furthest corner replied, "Sorry, sir, Major's orders are for constant monitoring, sir."

Everything stood still for a moment.

"Private Horton," said Sergeant Marker, and the name felt poisonous as it was spoken. "Major's orders have changed. You mean to say you know his mind better than I do? You don't want me to report you for insubordination, do you?"

"N-no, sir," the man replied, then quickly stood up from his chair and left, followed closely by the other private, who had been watching in bafflement at Horton's misstep.

Stephanie's heart sank. Not even the army seemed to be enough to thwart the Skaara's plan.

It wasn't until they were sure the soldiers were out of hearing range that the Chief pointed at the monitors. "Is that what we're working with?"

Marker gestured to follow him, then went to sit down in front of the surveillance monitors. "I can feed back yesterday's footage to the outside cameras, and you have your device to stop the recording on the inside," he explained. "All is under control, as long as you're out of there by sixteen-hundred when the new shift comes in."

"What about those three soldiers? How are you keeping them quiet?"

"Get me what I asked, and the boys won't be a problem."

"And what is it that you dare to ask?" interjected Stephanie, shooting her question like a poisonous dart.

The Chief's intervention was quick and calm. "I *offered* the sergeant," he explained, "the same implant you have granted me. I believe it will be beneficial to have extra eyes in the army once the mothership lands."

That was not good news for humanity. Not only the chief of a security agency, but also a sergeant of the actual army.

The Skaara, however, was not entirely satisfied. "Send your minion in here. That Victoria that makes terrible coffee. She will serve as surveillance on the sergeant."

Just as everybody's eyes were drawn away from the security screens, something caught Stephanie's attention. The Skaara was too preoccupied with assessing Marker to even notice. It was a moment, a shadow moving from left to right, from one tree to another.

She watched carefully, in case it happened again – in case it wasn't just a large animal watching from the undergrowth. So absorbed she was, it startled her to hear her own voice saying, "It won't take us long. We will be out in good time."

The Chief didn't bother nodding. He had been planning it all along, and Stephanie suspected the connection with the Skaara meant that he already knew most of what the alien knew. They were like twin siblings, except with a more accentuated hierarchy, a constant pressing of duties. She could feel the effort the Skaara was making to control an extra brain – it was giving her a headache.

Then there was that flicker again, on the same screen, somewhere by the edge of the perimeter fence. Nobody else noticed. The Chief and Marker were still talking.

"I recalled all the men that I could," the sergeant was saying, "but the two entrances are always guarded by at least one soldier. Nothing I could do about that."

The Chief shook his head. "It's not good enough, Sergeant."

"You are overestimating my authority around here, Edward."

"That's disappointing," interjected Stephanie.

In truth, it wasn't. The sergeant was, after all, reporting to his own superior officers – not that the Skaara would care about that, though.

Then the shadow appeared again, this time on a different screen, but still somewhere near the hangar. It lingered only for a second, enough for Stephanie to recognise his face.

Whatever reason Lucy's brother had to be at the landing site, she was sure it couldn't be to help the Skaara – not after all he had done to warn her against it.

"Maybe they can be convinced to move away?" the Chief suggested, clearly hinting at the Skaara doing the convincing.

"That might just be the case," the Skaara agreed, but she sounded distracted.

Stephanie's thought had started to seep through, and that had triggered all sorts of alarm bells.

She couldn't let the Skaara know about Frank's presence. She tried to stop the stream of thoughts as much as she could – or at least redirect it to more innocuous shores – while the alien scoured her mind. She started counting her breath, feeling its prying tentacles closing in, wondering if mindfulness exercises would be any use when it wasn't her mind in charge. Even in more ordinary circumstances, she had never been very good at it, and her thoughts quickly rushed in as she started making a mental list of topics she could focus on without giving away any useful information. It was a remarkably short list.

"If we're all set, I'd suggest you go, Edward," said Sergeant

Marker eventually. "The new shift comes in at sixteen-hundred, which gives you a full seven hours from now."

"Will you remain here for the full length?" the Chief asked.

The sergeant nodded. "I won't leave this tent until you're clear off site."

The grin was back on the Chief's face, creepy as a Chucky doll's smile. "Excellent. Let's get to work."

The hangar had been built around the spaceship when SafeOp Defence Services had been called to site. Because the hull was already taking up most of the clearing, the structure around it couldn't be much larger without incorporating birch and oak trees. As a result, the space inside was tight.

The personnel entrance – one of the only two doors to the hangar – was a person-sized rectangle in the corner of the structure. A single soldier was standing at attention in front of it. With all the confidence of a middle-aged white man in a position of power, the Chief walked up to him and showed his pass. "We're taking over, boy."

"I didn't receive the major's instruction, sir. With all due respect, you will not be taking over, sir."

The Chief exhaled and put the pass back in his breast pocket. "The hard way it is," he murmured, glancing up at the cameras.

Stephanie stepped closer, and the Skaara's grip grew weaker for a moment. She felt its tiny hooks moving against her back, then down her arm, which was now outstretched towards the soldier. He tried to step out of reach, but she was ready to catch him.

The soldier's eyes glazed over.

"Go fetch the other soldier, the one guarding the back. You two will be watching the front door together, and you'll let nobody come in after us."

136

The soldier nodded. When she let go of him, the Skaara crawled back up her arm and went to nest once again across her lower back.

As the soldier walked away, the full extent of that nightmare fell on Stephanie. Not only were the cameras blind, but the soldiers standing guard had been conditioned to obey the Skaara, while the alien hadn't lost control of Stephanie for one second. She found herself wondering how many in that base could be under the alien's conditioning, and if there was anyone who could be trusted in the least. She'd better assume not, if she wanted a chance to get out of there alive.

She wanted to believe that someone would soon figure out the fault in the surveillance system and barge into the hangar, at least providing backup, if not saving the day altogether. Maybe even Frank could have been able to raise the alarm. There wasn't much chance of that, though. Frank didn't even know they were there – and he wasn't a *Mission Impossible* type of guy anyway.

She thought things couldn't get any worse, until the Chief opened the small door, and she realised that the space inside the hangar was even tighter than she had anticipated.

One thing that she hadn't been able to overcome since being locked in the boot of her car was the fear of tight spaces. She knew all the techniques to keep that at bay, but something told her the Skaara wasn't going to let her use them.

Walking through the door, Stephanie felt the weight of the spaceship's presence, as the air compressed her throat. It was a couple of narrow metres between the hull and the walls, and they were rapidly closing in on her. She was aware that her breathing had become shallow, and the Skaara must have felt it too. Phobias were something even the alien couldn't manage so easily, apparently.

"I can't stay here," she managed to say.

The Chief had gone ahead to explore the side of the spaceship. He turned back with a puzzled look on his face. "Why not?"

His voice was floating and echoing around her. "I will be outside," she said, and she walked back, walls of blackness tunnelling her vision. She reached the door and emerged in the open air.

The bright light of day and the light breeze of the forest gave the world back to her. It was Stephanie again, for a moment. Only her. She gulped the vastness of the sky above her, and the musky air of the autumn woodland.

A soldier passed by and stopped to look at her. "You alright, ma'am?"

She turned to him. *That's my moment*, she thought. *If I could just warn him, maybe he could call the major and stop that madness.*

Then the Skaara swooped in, a moment before she could open her mouth to speak. Stephanie straightened up at once. "Of course. Everything is fine."

Another failed attempt. She wondered how many more she could take before she finally gave up.

"It's tight in there, I know," he continued.

"Have you been inside?" asked Stephanie. She could sense the Skaara was getting suspicious of the stranger.

"A couple of times, during inspections," the soldier replied. "Never alone, of course."

"Of course."

The soldier was a problem, even without Stephanie's cries for help.

"Lieutenant, weren't you on your way somewhere?" the

Chief's voice intervened as he emerged from the open door of the hangar. It was the Skaara's doing, no doubt about it. It was piloting the Chief like a radio-controlled toy car.

"Yes, sir," replied the soldier. "I was just checking on…" he trailed off, probably just realising he didn't know who she was.

"Agent Davis is perfectly fine, thank you," the Chief dismissed him. "I will take it from here."

The soldier frowned, unconvinced. "Sir, may I ask to see your pass to access the hangar?"

The Chief cocked his head at the request, as if he had been asked to produce a live rabbit from his hat. "What's your name, Lieutenant?"

"Rodner, sir."

He studied him for a second longer, then finally handed over his pass. "Very well, then. Have a look for yourself."

After a moment, Lieutenant Rodner handed back the plastic badge. "Apologies, sir. I didn't realise SafeOp was going to be on site today."

"No harm done," replied the Chief. "It's good to know we're all being cautious around this thing."

With something halfway between a salute and a wave, the soldier was back on his way. Stephanie watched him disappear behind the closest marquee, wishing she could scream at him to come back.

As the Chief walked back through the door, the Skaara steered Stephanie into the hangar as well.

Knowing what to expect didn't help soften the impact. Her vision went blurry as soon as the door closed behind her. She knew her throat was tightening again, but the Skaara didn't seem to care. If she had been in control of her own body – of her own breathing – she would've known how to deal with it, how to placate the panic. The alien, however, wasn't giving her a chance.

She leaned against the spaceship wall while her breathing intensified and tunnel vision set in, her feet stumbling on the uneven ground. The Skaara guided her to an abandoned shelving unit.

Stephanie's eyes locked on a pair of handcuffs that had been laid down on one of the shelves. She knew what was coming, but all the kicking and fussing she did in her head wasn't enough to prevent it.

The Skaara had work to do. It couldn't watch over her the whole time.

She was powerless as she watched her own hands working to secure the handcuffs to the metallic bars of the shelving unit on one side, and to her wrist on the other.

Feeling the alien crawling down her leg and away from her, she slid back into her own body. It was more painful than she had expected. The Skaara had found new skin to grapple on, making it feel as if an inexperienced tattoo artist was trying to decorate the entire surface all at once. That wasn't the worst part, though.

With the Skaara off her back, Stephanie was left battling the waves of panic at their peak. Her throat was so tight, she was barely breathing, her legs turned to jelly, and she had to lean heavily against the shelves so as not to collapse.

She closed her eyes and breathed in, telling herself to calm down, that she knew what to do. It took a while to take her mind off the brink of the abyss and ground herself in the moment. When she opened her eyes again, her own hand appeared surprisingly in focus, while her ears filled with the loud noise of her own blood flowing.

She was faintly aware of minutes passing, yet her mind was still blurry. It was hard to focus on anything at all. Even the spaceship in front of her, as huge and imposing as it was, seemed to be easily forgettable.

When the Chief reappeared next to her, she hadn't even seen him coming. He was carrying a gun.

"You're going to shoot me?" she managed to say. She heard her own voice distant, muffled.

He looked puzzled. "Of course not. This is for you."

As if that made more sense. Stephanie straightened up, and something about having her spine upright made her head wobble. "What do you mean?"

"It's a new issue," he explained as he turned it around, proudly showing off his new toy. "Entirely non-lethal, but it knocks a man out in one shot and less than five seconds. Just be sure to aim close to the heart. Or the head, if that's your preference."

"I can knock you out with my own gun, and that'd be permanent."

He raised his eyebrows at her, then reached forward to take Stephanie's gun from the holster, looking confident that she wasn't going to do anything to stop him – and she didn't. "You don't sound as threatening as you think when you can barely stand, you know?"

He was right. Stephanie would have been on the ground already if it hadn't been for the shelving unit holding her up.

"Why are you giving this to me, then?" she asked, nodding at the tranquiliser.

"I have to leave for a short time. The van needs to be organised to be picked up. You will shoot anybody who walks in through that door."

It wasn't a request. He knew she was going to do it.

He pointed towards the entrance, and Stephanie felt like a ten-year-old being told how to play videogames by her grandfather. "Why does the Skaara need a van?"

The Chief glanced at the spaceship and gestured for her to step aside. "Move along. I'll show."

As if on cue, a whirring noise came from the spaceship. It was just around the corner, so it was difficult for Stephanie to see what was going on, but she felt something changing around her, as if the air had all at once filled with static.

She shuffled aside, her arm stretching from the handcuffs. Her left shoulder burst into stars of pain, while a wave of adrenaline brought her mind to sudden focus. She twisted her grip in the attempt to find some relief.

When she looked up at the spaceship, a panel was hanging off the wall. The light coming from the inside had a purple and orange tinge to it. Only part of the hull was visible to her, but the floor seemed covered in pods the size and shape of footballs.

"What are those things?"

"Pods, capsules, containers, pick the name you like the most." He sounded like a proud father as he said that. Stephanie wondered how much of the Chief was left, and how much of his brain had already turned Skaara.

"You mean like eggs?"

"No, not like that. They're not carrying anything living. It's all about preparing for the mothership's landing."

Mothership. He had mentioned it earlier in the surveillance marquee, Stephanie remembered. She tried to figure out what that all meant, but keeping her mind focussed felt like soldiering on through a calculus class, staring at a jumble of weird symbols, nodding along at the professor's mysterious puns while her classmates were throwing paper planes at her. "Gwyn is a scout," she managed.

"You remember her name," he commented.

"You're making me," she replied. It was true. The memory of the name was branded in her memory. The Skaara clearly didn't like being considered *alien*. "That's why you need the van, to get the pods out of here," she continued. Speaking her mind out loud was helping her put things together, string them in line. "That's why you need Lucy."

"It sounds like you were really looking forward to meeting her yourself," he replied, an unexpected hint of mockery in his voice. "It's nothing personal. We just don't trust you, and Gwyn can't leave the premises yet. There's too much to get ready."

He walked back to her and slid the tranquiliser gun into her holster in place of the one he had taken away. "Stay put while I'm away," he said, then left her.

By the time Stephanie had unholstered the gun and raised her arm to aim at him, he was already out of sight.

She turned to the pods, trying to lean as far as she could to have a better look. The Skaara was crawling around like a small monkey swinging between branches.

Stephanie shuffled to a more comfortable position, then folded down, face inches from the ground, her back tingling with each breath.

If she could have shot the wretched thing when she had the chance, the world would have been safe. If she had shot the Chief before he sprung his trap, she would have at least gotten better odds. She could've stopped him from opening the backpack. She could have fought him then. She could've said she had seen the Skaara, even when she hadn't. She would've been safe, and so would the world.

She hadn't done any of that.

Her body sank lower until her forehead touched the ground.

- XI -

His eyes fixed on the road ahead, Matthew gripped the steering wheel as if worried he was going to be catapulted out of the car at any moment.

It had been easy for Lucy to convince him to pick her up. He still felt guilty for leaving her and Frank at the mercy of those SafeOp goons.

It took a bit more inventiveness to persuade him to drive to his parents' house in the Cotswolds, a one-hour drive out of town, as opposed to his cosy flat share in Bristol only fifteen minutes down the road. She couldn't quite tell him that a space crawler had given her instructions to steal his father's toys, so she made up some desperate need to be away from the crowd instead. When she started saying how he was the only person she felt safe with, he finally stopped resisting.

"I'm just a bit surprised, that's all," Matthew said. "I guess part of me thought I'd never hear from you again."

"Oh, I thought of that," Lucy replied. "I mean, you did dump us with a bunch of MI6-style goons and ran for the hills." She knew there was a better response she could have given, but her mind was somewhere else.

Below the darkening sky, Lucy watched the fields line up on the horizon. She hoped he would desist in his attempt to explain himself and leave her alone with her thoughts.

He didn't. "Did Frank get out too? I haven't heard from him."

She forced her attention on the conversation, even if her heart wasn't in it. "He must have gone home. I'm going to check on him in the morning, anyway. I'll tell him you said hi."

"Should I come with you?" he offered. "I have a meeting at lunch, but I'm sure I can sort something out and move it."

Not an option, she thought. *Not this time.* "Thanks. It's probably better if I see him alone."

Matthew took his eyes off the road for the first time, even if for only a moment. "Why? Is there something wrong with him? Did that alien thing mess him up or something?"

"It's called Skaara, that alien thing. And no, it's not that."

"Whatever you want to call it, it's an alien thing," he grunted.

She decided to ignore his hostility. "We've been secluded for weeks, Frank and I, while you went on with your life. You have to give him some time to adjust."

He exhaled his disgruntlement. "Listen, I said I'm sorry. My father took me out; there wasn't much I could do about it."

Words flew out of Lucy's mouth before she could realise it. "You could've stood up to him."

"You guys went to touch the bloody alien thing!" he burst, probably voicing his frustration for the first time in weeks. He exhaled before adding, "Even if I had convinced my dad, he still couldn't have gotten you out as well."

"Then maybe you could've stayed with us, instead of riding off into the sunset," she fired back.

The silence that followed was electric. Her comment was unfair, and she knew it. He didn't say anything, and she wasn't going to apologise.

Eventually, she decided to break the silence. "For real,

though. Would you be able to give me a lift to see Frank tomorrow?" She meant it as a peace offering and crossed her fingers, hoping he would take it as such.

Matthew stole a glance at her. He didn't look keen, until finally he exhaled and nodded. "Of course, I'll take you," he agreed. "Will you need picking up as well?"

She didn't even know what they were going to ask her to do, let alone if she was going to need a ride back. All things considered, flying saucers could be hovering over Great Britain by the afternoon. "Maybe. I'll let you know."

Lucy allowed herself a silent breath of relief. He was exceptionally kind-hearted, and so diametrically different from her, which was what made him a much better person than she was. Lucy still wondered how he managed that, considering the family of snobs he grew up in.

By then, they were turning onto the access road to Partridge Manor. Lucy had only heard about it until then. She straightened up to gaze through the trees, trying to get a glimpse of the house. After a sharp bend in the road, the headlights reflected against the ground floor windows. Then the sensor lights came on, and the full arrogance of the place revealed itself.

Matthew's family had made it their favourite game to make themselves look so wealthy that most people around them would feel like beggars. It was still puzzling how they had managed to raise a good person like Matthew. She almost felt bad about dragging him into that mess.

Once the car was parked in the driveway, they made their way inside. Right away, the inside of the manor revealed itself to be just as pretentious as the exterior was. Everything was made of solid wood, there was a grand piano in the corner to the left, and the stairs to the first floor were as wide as a small country road and ended in a balcony overlooking the entrance. As if all that wasn't pompous enough, the Cavell's had added one final personal touch in the shape of a huge family portrait hanging opposite the front door, there to judge all those who dared walk in.

The stairs to the first floor took the left side of the room, while Matthew led her to the right through a small door and straight to the kitchen. Even when he turned on the light, the dark wood of the surfaces seemed to keep the room in shadow.

Lucy took a seat at the side of a large table, while Matthew went to check the cupboard.

"Did you say you haven't eaten since you left that place?" he asked, handing her a pack of crisps.

"Yep, and that was breakfast," she said, thinking it better not to mention her stop at Davis' house and the cream crackers. She ripped the pack open and shoved half of its contents in her mouth, immediately regretting the image she was presenting of herself.

She noticed him hiding an amused smile while surveying the freezer. "There's not much choice of food. Nobody was supposed to come here for another couple of months."

She stood up to check the rest of the cupboards, while Matthew closed the freezer. She found a pack of salt and pepper crackers and showed it to him.

"Is that going to be enough?" he asked.

"It's food," she said with a sigh. "As long as you promise me there'll be breakfast in the morning."

"What about we get breakfast on the way to your brother?" he offered.

It was his attempt to make it up to her. She smiled at him. "Sure."

* * *

She woke up with a start. It took her a moment to remember where she was.

It was still dark outside. Matthew was sleeping peacefully by her side. Even the morning birds hadn't started chirping yet, and it felt like the world outside was still fast asleep, just like everyone and everything in the whole of Partridge Manor. Except for her, that was.

Lucy got up from the bed and silently stretched. A night's sleep in a decent bed hadn't cured her of her nightmares but at least had done some good to her lower back.

She wrapped herself in the warm fabric of the fancy dressing gown she had been given, then sneaked out of the room.

There was a bathroom at the end of the hall, and the cabinet below the sink was stocked with all sorts of pills a human could wish for. Her hand hovered over the codeine for a moment, then thought better of it.

She grabbed the box of aspirin instead, took two on the spot, and dropped the rest in the pocket of the dressing gown.

Out of the bathroom, she made her way down the hall and the stairs. Cook's text instructed her to find Mr Cavell's study.

Once on the ground floor, however, the appearance of the kitchen door was a ruthless reminder for an empty stomach. She could spare a minute, she decided, although the fridge was indeed as desolate as Matthew had described it the night before. The cupboard hadn't improved either. She grabbed a box of cereal. She would have made coffee, but that was probably overkill.

Down the hall, the parlour was to be her next step. Even in

the dim light of her smartphone's torch, it was the depiction of pretentiousness. She could almost imagine Mr and Mrs Cavell sitting down with their wealthy guests, the room full of cigar smoke, and a fully stocked liquor cabinet at the ready.

There was a door past the chairs. She went to open it, and, sure enough, the library was nudged right behind it. It wasn't big, but it was impressive. She aimed the flash light at the ceiling-high shelves filled with dusty tomes and golf trophies. Running her fingers along the smooth spine of Proust's *In Search Of Lost Time*, she was sure nobody had ever opened any of them.

Another door stood to the far side of the room. Lucy was ready to guess that was the one she was looking for.

She silently closed the door behind her and flashed the torch around. In the small room, the large desk dominated the space, while the walls were covered with pictures of Mr Cavell smiling and waving with his big-name friends. Behind the desk and between two large windows was the reproduction of Vermeer's Flemish girl, with her absurdly elongated red hat. The frame was way smaller than she had expected.

She was about to move the frame when she heard a scraping sound coming from the floor above. Matthew must have woken up.

The house went quickly back to silence. It was too late to back away, and it was only going to take a minute anyway. Keeping an ear out for any suspicious movement, Lucy went to analyse the frame. As she lifted it from the wall, the safe appeared behind it. How original.

The code hadn't been difficult to memorise – Matthew's birthday, one removed. Still, she held her breath when she pressed enter. The mechanism clicked open, and it was the best sound in the whole wide world. It always was.

A small black box was all she could see inside. Cook's message hadn't been too specific on what she would find, and she wasn't expecting diamonds for sure.

More shuffling from upstairs meant Matthew was by then looking around and wondering where she went. She had no time to figure out what it was that she was looking at. She grabbed the black box, closed the safe, cleaned the handle and painting frame of her prints, then sneaked back to the kitchen to put the cereal box where she found it, lest Matthew find out about her early snack.

By the time she made it back to the room, the country birds had started celebrating the brightening of the morning sky. Matthew was sitting on the bed, checking his phone. He dropped it on the bedcover as soon as he saw her. "Is everything okay?"

"Yeah, just needed the bathroom," she lied. Then, she thought to add, "I took some aspirin from your mum's stash. I hope that's okay."

"Sure. Is it your back still?" he asked.

She nodded as she went to sit next to him. "Are you going to have a shower?"

He chuckled. "Is this your polite way of telling me I need one?"

"You know I'm not that polite," she teased him. She did need the room, though. "I'm just being practical. We have to leave soon, and you have to get ready."

She leaned closer and rested her head on his shoulder. He gently wrapped his arm around her and kissed her forehead. "Ever so sensible," he replied softly. "You can use my mother's shower. Her room is just opposite if you want a change of clothes."

She nodded against his chest, then pulled away as she prodded him. "Go."

He chuckled again and walked out of the room. It was such a good feeling to make him laugh that way.

Finally alone, Lucy took the black box from her pocket. It looked like one of those Chinese puzzles, where the pressure on one specific point was going to open the whole thing up. She had never been good at solving those. Frank was the puzzle guy

She put the box aside and started her phone. The lock screen told her it was twenty past seven. She sent a text message to Frank, knowing he was going to be awake and waiting.

I'm with Matt. Probs a few days. Let the army deal with the crawly invaders.

It was important she got him to stand down. She needed him as far away from the Skaara as possible, until she found a way to put the space crawler out of business.

While waiting for her brother's reply, she opened the Google Maps on her phone. The address that Davis had given her was for a business park in the middle of the Wye Valley, miles away from Frank's home. She had to come up with a pretty good excuse to drive all the way there.

Navigating the area on the small screen of her smartphone was painfully uncomfortable. For a second she almost wished she could spread one of those paper maps over the bed, then remembered herself.

She spotted a forest centre nearby the location. The online map said it would have been a ten minutes' walk to the business park via a footpath. *It'd better be right*, she thought.

Lucy was about to check opening times when a soft knock came from the door. "Hey, you still in there? I'm going to make coffee."

"You're a life saver," she called out. "I'll be down in five."

She heard the shuffling of feet moving away from the door. She gave herself a minute to gather her thoughts before crossing the hall to Mrs Cavell's room. She picked the most inconspicuous top and some clean underwear. A fancy leather jacket caught her eye, but she eventually decided to stick with her own – she regretfully had to admit that all those pockets came in handy.

When she finally made it downstairs, Matthew was waiting for her in the kitchen. "I see you found my mother's yoga outfit," he said, pointing at her top.

"It was this or a satin cocktail dress. Not my style."

He smiled, handing her a fresh mug of coffee. "I wouldn't have complained."

Lucy smiled in return and took a sip from the mug. Not sweet. "Do the mighty Cavell have some sugar?"

He shook his head. "Couldn't find any. Is it that bad?"

"Nah, it's fine."

It was horrible. Still, the stale cereals had dried up her mouth, making it easier to pretend she was enjoying the bitter brew.

He was already washing his mug. "You take your time," he said as he placed it on the rack to dry. "I'll go get my stuff. We'll go as soon as you're ready."

"Mattie," she called before he could leave the room. She bit her lip. "I don't think we'll have time to stop for breakfast."

A puzzled expression appeared on his face. "Why's that?"

She looked down at her coffee. "We're not going to Frank's place."

The look on his face was worse than disappointment, his warm smile all but vanished.. "And where is it that you need to go?"

"It's a place in the Wye Valley."

He exhaled, and she could see that he was going to take her anyway, even if it was going to be extremely unpractical for him. "Luce, that's forty minutes away from here at least, and the opposite direction from where I've got to go. Is that where Frank is? What is he doing there?"

Lucy shrugged. "Don't know, didn't ask. Walks in the woods, I guess."

"What, to see if he can find some more of those space things?"

She exhaled. "Matt, please."

He sighed and nodded. "Fine, but you haven't eaten since yesterday morning. You said so yourself. We should stop to get something."

"Yeah, I know," she said slowly. She was still hungry after all.

"I should get my stuff anyway," he concluded. "We better leave soon."

"Thank you," said Lucy as he walked away. She exhaled. She knew she was pushing his patience a bit harder than usual. As long as he drove that morning, she decided she could patch things up later – if there was even going to be a later, since the Skaara takeover was on the afternoon program.

A few minutes later, they were ready to go, with the car's navigation system set to take them to the forest centre.

It was like starting off on an adventure that had begun three weeks earlier. The small puzzle box was tucked in an inside pocket of Lucy's jacket. The flash drive sloth was safely reattached to her keys in her left pocket, together with the box of painkillers. A deep frown of disappointment was carved onto Matthew's face.

As they drove past cottage houses and sheep pastures, the radio was the only one talking, until Lucy couldn't take the atmosphere anymore. "I'm sorry," she forced herself to say, knocking her pride to the side for once.

He turned the radio down. "For what?"

"I'm not trying to make it hard for you. I'm just worried about Frankie. It was a difficult few weeks in that place." *It wasn't technically a lie*, she told herself.

Matthew's frown softened a little. "We can still get a coffee and a sausage roll on the way."

"I was thinking maybe a bacon bap," she replied.

He chuckled at that. "You're impossible."

The bacon bap wasn't hard to find. They ate by the car with an eye on the time, while Lucy tried her best to look interested in whatever Matthew's meeting was going to mean for the Cavell family – some big endeavour, government deals and whatnot. As if he needed the job anyway, when Dad's monthly allowance was enough to cover a small town's salary. If it had been her, she would have been sitting around all day, reading books, watching films, and ordering takeout.

It was worth enduring the conversation, though. The chance of breakfast together boosted both of their spirits and finally filled the hole in Lucy's stomach.

When they arrived at the forest centre, Matthew wasn't content with her alone there. "I can't see Frank. Do you want to call him?"

"He's probably just sitting on a bench further in," she said, waving him away.

She checked her phone. Frank hadn't replied to her text yet. She wished she could go check on him for real.

Matthew still didn't seem persuaded but didn't protest any

further. "Just give me a ring if you need me to come and get you."

She nodded and kissed him lightly on the lips, then got out of the car and watched him sit there, punching new coordinates in his phone. The lies she was telling him were stacking up at an alarming rate. If it went on that way, she'd have to start taking notes.

Her mind back to business, she quickly figured out that the walk to the meeting with Davis was going to take her way more than ten minutes, since the footpath through the green field was still soaked in mud from the previous day's rain. She regretted not taking Mrs Cavell's boots. In her flimsy trainers, she had no choice but to take the main road, which arched around the town.

At least it's not raining anymore, she thought, watching the dark clouds gathering on the horizon. *Not yet.*

When she arrived at the business centre, there were barely any cars around. She checked for motorcycles, like the one Davis had been riding when she took the space crawler from her – the same one she had seen parked in front of her home. None was in sight. It looked like motorcycle season was already over.

Maybe Lucy was early. Or Davis was late, if that was even possible.

She leaned against the wall, and the pain in her lower back came knocking once again. Straightening up wasn't enough to relieve the pressure, she knew, and yoga stretches in the parking lot were out of the question, even if she somehow remembered which were the good ones for her. She fished in her pocket for the aspirin tablets and took two.

Cook showed himself from round the corner of the home

furniture store. *That's not right*, Lucy thought. She glanced around one more time just in case Davis was hiding in one of the cars, but Cook was clearly the intended hook-up.

She felt the mysterious box pressing against her ribs as she dug her hands deep into her pockets, wrapping her fingers around the fuzzy sloth. If things went sideways, those two items were the best insurance she had, and she didn't even know what was contained in either of them.

Their eyes met. Cook stepped away and turned the corner as soon as Lucy started walking towards him. She followed him to the delivery area at the back of the store, where the solid presence of fried chicken in the air made her hungry all over again. There must have been a fast-food place nearby. She was going to find it later.

Cook had stopped by the side of a van, waiting for her to join him. "You look disappointed," he said by way of greeting.

"I'm not," she replied. *Disappointment* wasn't the right word for it. "Are you going to expand on the threat to my brother, or is it just another favour you're asking?"

"It's only with my help that you haven't been arrested yet. To make it a fair exchange of services, you owe me one."

How pedantic, and most annoying since he was technically right, which made Lucy want to kick him in the shin even more. "Not my fault if you can't keep your minions under control, so if I had been arrested, it still would have been your fault," she snarled, pushing the insolence level up to a hundred. "I got you out of there, didn't I? That was the deal. Also, you do know that I'm the only person you can trust without brainwashing. If you lose me, your manpower is down by a third. Are you factoring that in?"

"Is this your best attempt at threatening me?"

Lucy stared at him for a whole three seconds. Yes, that was her best attempt. A pretty rubbish one.

He eventually shrugged and asked, "Did you get the box?"

"Mattie wouldn't let me out of his sight," she said quickly. "You know, he's been waiting for me to get out of quarantine, and boys have their needs."

Cook's vacant stare told her the Skaara did not really know what she meant. "You don't have the box," he commented.

"I know where it is." Then she added, "And you told me Davis was going to be here. Instead of her pretty smile, I get your ugly face. I guess we're even."

"I thought you said you weren't disappointed."

Lucy recoiled. "I'm not," she repeated, unsure why it felt like she was lying. Better to change the subject, she decided. "What's in that box that's so important anyway? And why is it with Matt's parents?"

"That would be none of your business," he replied, then shrugged and waved at the van behind him. "Can you drive this?"

"You mean legally? You already know I don't have a licence."

"I mean practically."

Lucy considered the van. She had driven smaller vehicles; driving that thing wasn't going to be much different. It was four wheels and an engine, after all. "Sure," she said.

"Bring it to the landing site today at midday," he ordered. "You'll go through the delivery access route. A map of the site and your pass are both on the passenger seat."

Lucy peaked through the driver's window and spotted a clipboard carrying a few notes and a pass card. Underneath was a folded map of the area – how old-fashioned. The keys were already in the ignition.

"Any questions?" asked Cook, clearly eager to close the meeting.

Yes, actually. A lot of questions. It was a surprise even to Lucy when the first one that came to mind was, "How's Agent Davis?"

She turned to look at Cook when he didn't reply. The smirk on his face was the creepiest thing she had seen yet.

That's what I get for worrying about other human beings.

"Yesterday she seemed in distress," she explained. "If she's not here today, does that mean you lost control of one of your toys?"

The smirk on Cook's face disappeared. Lucy made a mental note of that, then opened the van and took the driver seat. As she went to close the door, Cook grabbed the side to hold it open. "You bring the van to the hangar at midday, and stop worrying about my agents," he said. Then, in a whisper, "And pray nobody realises what you're doing there before you get out. You're not as irreplaceable as you think."

- XII -

It felt like hours since the Chief had left. Yet, when Stephanie
checked her watch, it had only been forty-five minutes.

A few times the Skaara had appeared in her line of sight, as
if taunting her, knowing that she couldn't take the shot. After
a while, Stephanie had laid down the weapon and just sat on
the ground, her back against the wall, right arm hanging limp
from the handcuffs.

She had tried standing a couple of times, but her head had
started swimming, the rashes on her back brushing against the
wall as she sank to her haunches, making it feel as if her skin
was bursting into flames.

Even that pain, however, wasn't enough to snap her mind
into focus. She had started to believe that the Skaara was
responsible for the fuzziness just as much as the claustrophobia
was. That being the case or not, she had to find a way out.
Because there was always a way out.

She tried to focus on the shelves and the space around her, in
the hope she might find something she could use to free herself.
No luck, though. The place had been swiped clean. It made her
wonder why the shelf alone had been left there at all.

Maybe she should have just shot herself. That way the Skaara
couldn't have used her as a ride anymore. Then again, it wasn't

160

going to be difficult for that thing to find another human to reduce to a puppet.

She weighed the gun in her hand for a few seconds, then placed it back in her lap, ready in case something else appeared that was worth shooting.

Her head was drifting into improbable escape plans when the back door opened and the Chief reappeared. He looked happier than ever. Stephanie's heart sank.

"Your girlfriend says hi," he mocked from a distance.

She frowned, trying to connect the dots. That had to be the alien's idea of a joke. He must have met Lucy. Stephanie's spirit took a new dive.

After checking the Skaara's progress with the pods – whatever progress he needed to check, as they were literally sharing a brain – he walked over to her, then leaned on the shelving to lower himself to be eye level with her. His conspiratorial stance made her want to spit in his face.

She looked straight ahead, avoiding his gaze, while her hand gripped the gun tighter, finger lingering on the trigger.

"I know what you're thinking. That someone will come in here and find out what we're doing. That they'll set you free and save your world, isn't that right?"

"Are you here to tell me your masterplan?" she asked through gritted teeth.

It was as if Stephanie had just served him a slice of lemon. "Your allegiance is to humankind, we understand that," he said, "but there is no avoiding the mothership landing. You attempt at resistance is completely futile."

She grimaced. "Okay, now you sound like a cheap movie character."

"Your taunting is not going to keep you alive."

"No, but it passes the time. Plus, you say I'm hopeless, yet you're still keeping me handcuffed. Am I that dangerous to you?"

He replied with a scoff, "Don't flatter yourself." He stood up and started walking away.

"I could shoot you right now with the same gun you gave me. Have you thought about that?" she shouted at his back.

"Do you think that would make a difference?" He didn't bother turning towards her, and his voice sounded as if coming from another planet.

No, she thought, *but it would be very satisfying.* She raised the gun at him just as he turned all the way to face her. He stood there, waiting for her to go through with her threat.

She was sure she could take the shot, right to his head. He was only a few metres away, and her hand was steady–

Until it was not.

As the barrel of the gun aligned with the Chief's forehead, Stephanie's whole body started trembling at the effort. She resisted as much as she could, putting all her strength in her index finger, but it was too much. Her arm fell back into her lap.

"What have you done to me?" she managed.

There was a hint of pride in the Chief's tone when he said, "The human brain is such an interesting tool to play with."

He then disappeared round the corner of the spaceship. The last bit of hope that Stephanie was holding fell apart right then.

Rock bottom or not, it wasn't a place where Stephanie liked to linger. For the third time, she grabbed at the shelving unit and lifted herself up from the ground. Her head began to float, and her vision closed in, so she closed her eyes with it, watching her own breath, holding on to the metal frame as it was the only thing keeping her upright.

During years of missions, nothing had ever made her so helpless. She leaned back against the wall, prodding her legs in a desperate effort not to sink down again, while trying to find an angle that wouldn't worsen the already sore skin on her back.

Head tilted back, she kept her eyes closed, feeling the blood rush to her handcuffed hand. For a few moments, the rest of the world slowly drifted away from her.

It could have been ten of fifty minutes later when the back door of the hangar closed with a loud bang, bringing Stephanie back to her senses. She looked around. Nobody was in sight.

The brief pause had done her some good, and her mind was feeling clearer. She wished the Chief would come into sight, to test if the alien's sway was wearing off already.

When the door opened again, Stephanie gripped the gun. She was probably going to have only one shot, if any. She raised her aim, ready to fire, then froze.

Lucy was standing with her hands up, staring straight at the weapon. "Good to see you too, darling," she said, with half a smile. "Not sure I'm liking this tradition we're making. I'm not a fan of being held at gunpoint."

It still made sense to take the shot, she told herself. Stephanie's finger lingered on the trigger for a moment, then she lowered the gun. "You brought the van," she surmised.

"You got yourself handcuffed," replied Lucy as she walked closer. She was studying Stephanie's figure as if looking for something. "No offense, but you look like shit."

"Not funny."

"A little bit."

Stephanie found herself smiling despite herself. "Well, I

wouldn't recommend alien possession as a beauty treatment."

Lucy's eyes widened as she went serious. She glanced around, then said, "The space crawler, where did it go?"

She nodded towards the spaceship. "In there."

The girl leaned backwards to catch a glimpse of it, but the wall was sealed once again. "What's it doing?"

There wasn't a useful answer she could give, and there wasn't any time to talk about motherships and pods anyway. Something else was way more important. "Listen, I need you to get me out of these handcu-"

Lucy's hand was on her mouth before she could finish the word, holding her silent and pressing her against the wall. Stephanie winced at the pain that caused.

"Are you hurt?" asked Lucy.

She wasn't going to answer that.

Lucy leaned in closer, warm breath to her ear. "Just keep quiet, okay?" she whispered. "You do that, and maybe nobody dies."

They stared at each other for a long moment. There was something oddly reassuring in that closeness, even if everything about Lucy looked like the shiniest red flag. Stephanie couldn't even figure out if her words were meant to be a warning, a threat, or a heartfelt piece of advice.

She nodded her understanding. Lucy let go and made to leave.

Not yet, Stephanie thought. She grabbed Lucy by the arm and pulled her back. They were face to face again, inches apart.

"What the fuck, Davis?" whispered Lucy. It sounded like an earnest question.

"Your brother. He's here," she whispered back.

Lucy frowned, then pulled away again. She hadn't known. "How do you know that? Where is he?"

"Security cameras caught him this morning. I have no idea what he's doing here, or where he's gone."

A loud clang came from outside, and Lucy's head turned in alarm. "Shit," she let out.

The last glance the girl threw at Stephanie seemed almost pleading, as if she was begging her to save her brother. Stephanie wished she could.

Watching Lucy leave the hangar, Stephanie wanted to believe she had made the right call.

If she was right about her, the girl was likely helping the Skaara only because she was under threat. Maybe Lucy would find a way to get her brother to safety. Maybe she could even sabotage the alien's plan and help prevent the invasion.

Just as likely, Lucy was going to do anything the Skaara asked her to do, if that meant keeping herself and Frank alive.

Stephanie exhaled. It was possible she had just made a terrible mistake and doomed not only herself, but all of humankind.

- XIII -

The spaceship looked so much smaller in the hangar. Lucy remembered finding it in the clearing, and how it took up her whole field of vision. It was odd to think there was a box big enough to contain it, yet there it was – and there was still space to walk around it. Not much, but still.

The electricity in the air, instead, was exactly like she remembered.

Davis was the one who delivered the real surprise, and not by getting herself handcuffed to a bunch of shelves – Lucy had seen that one coming. Learning that her brother was there had been much more alarming. She had to find him, understand what the hell he was doing there, and send him home with a *thank you but no thank you* card. Bonus points if she managed to avoid the lecture about the amorality of aiding an alien invasion, as if she wasn't doing it to save his skin. All of that, of course, with neither Cook nor the Skaara catching a glimpse of him. Easy.

"Here's our thief."

Speak of the devil, thought Lucy. She turned around to see Cook walking towards her. She would have punched that grin off his face if she could have. His cheerfulness felt like a maniac's laugh before throwing puppies into a meat grinder.

"Mr Space General," she called back with her best attempt at a smile. "What a pleasure being called a thief in the middle of an army camp."

He placed a hand on her shoulder as soon as he was close enough to do so. She wished she could knee him in the groin. "We were expecting you," he said.

"You don't say," she replied. "You told me to come, remember? The whole *meet me behind the fried chicken place, take the van, and come at midday*?"

That must have been the Skaara's effect on his brain. Either that, or the space crawlers were the most thespian beings in the universe. Lucy found herself checking the side of his head, to see if there was any grey matter trickling out of his ears, just in case.

Quite possibly he hadn't even heard her comment, as he declared, "I want to show you something."

He pulled more than guided her, keeping her close enough for her to drown in his aftershave. She could have gripped his gun, if she wanted – too bad she had no idea how to shoot with it.

They walked past Davis, and around the spacecraft, all the way to the other side, where a breach the size of a letterbox was letting out a purple and orange light. It was an awful colour combo. Lucy was sure it was the same breach that had opened in front of them when they had first found the ship.

She stopped a few feet away, resisting even when Cook insisted on pulling her forward. "What is that light?" she asked him.

"You're scared of it."

Lucy gave him a sideway glance. "Not scared," she said. "Wary. I've seen some shit since this thing landed, remember?"

167

He ignored the comment and knocked by the side of the purple light opening. After a moment, the wall caved in on itself and opened wide.

She stepped further away at the sight of the ship's cargo. Stills of spider-like creatures grabbing at people's faces flashed through her mind.

Beside her, Cook burst out laughing. "So much for not being scared."

"What are these for?" she asked. *Please don't say eggs*, she thought to herself.

"Supplies. Groundwork, mostly," he replied as he stepped inside the hull.

Not eggs. Lucy did her best to hide the relief.

She glanced around the hull interior. Bathed in the oddly coloured light, the walls and ceiling were covered with hooks and nooks, probably designed for optimised crawling in zero gravity. As if giving a demonstration, the Skaara was dangling over the cargo, limbs sprawled across three different holds. Occupying the floor of the hull were something between fifteen and twenty egg-shaped pods, maybe more. All of them together could fit easily in the van. It was a delivery job, then. As long as Mama Skaara had given her blessing, Lucy reckoned she was going to be fine.

"Where am I supposed to take them?"

"You'll know in due course," replied Cook. "First, you will load them onto the van."

Easy. "That's it?"

"Each of them is locked to the hull for safe storage. You'll have to release the magnetic grip for each one of them."

She could have expected as much from interstellar travel. "How do I do that, then? Is there a button? Or do I just pull really hard?"

She watched him kneel by the closest one and start working at its base, kneading the soft spongy material in an almost disturbing way. "Why are you massaging the pod?"

Instead of replying, Cook quit handling the foamy base and gently pulled until the pod came unstuck with a loud suction sound. He held it up base-first, showing the concave bottom.

"The soft matter at the base is only a protection," he explained. "The pods are tightened to the surface and need to be disengaged before they can be removed."

She nodded. "Got it. Unstick the sticky stuff, then pull until it comes off. Should be fine."

What a sensible way to transport fragile items through space.

Slowly, she lifted her foot and stepped inside. It was quite an uneventful step. The soft electrical buzz became a bit stronger, true, but everything else felt quite unremarkable. No force field, no booby traps, not even the slightest hint at some greater force pulling at her subconscious. Almost disappointing.

Cook had noticed her hesitation. "The spaceship is not going to wrap itself around you, nor throw you into fits, if that's what you're expecting."

She hadn't realised he had been staring. "Well, you never know. Lower your guard one minute and your brain becomes minced meat for space crawlers."

She knew he caught the reference when he glared at her. She was maybe walking a thin line there, but she couldn't help it. When she made to move past him to get the next pod, he grabbed her arm and stopped her mid-step.

"You'll get the van first. Have it ready by the door," he said, the tone of his voice as firm as the grip of his hand. "Each pod goes in, close the door, and come back to get the next one. We can't risk anybody seeing."

Lucy fought the impulse to headbutt him. "You're saying I shouldn't wave at the cameras? I thought you had a magic pen for that sort of thing."

"Surveillance is not the issue," he replied, letting go of her arm.

She pulled her hand to her chest, as if he was going to snatch it away again. She didn't like his touch, and she didn't like orders. Not to mention, closed doors made for a poor escape route if things got out of hand. She felt the urge to leave every door open in her wake, even those she didn't have to walk through.

On the other hand, she was in no position to bargain. She headed straight out, only to stop just outside the door after slamming it closed behind her. It was getting harder by the minute to suffer the Skaara's presumptuous attitude. It was only for a little longer, she told herself. Long term benefit. Survival and all that.

The van was parked by the side of the hangar, nudged between trees that coasted the clearing. She walked towards it, checking the surroundings for Frank's presence. There was no sign of him. If he was hanging around there, he must have found a very good hiding spot.

It was a tight squeeze between the hangar and the trees, and mostly littered with bits of wood and scraps of metal. Adding to the dumping-grounds feeling, the grass carried a yellowish hue, when it was there at all – such was the effect of an army camp on a forest.

There wasn't much space to manoeuvre, and she still wasn't used to the bulky size of the vehicle. She swivelled the van around and all seemed well, until a screeching metallic sound made her hit the brakes. She checked the rear-view mirror. A tree branch was pressing against the left side of the vehicle.

Lucy exhaled a small curse, then turned the wheel and moved away from the tree, adjusted course, and managed to get to the back entrance of the hangar without any further incident. Once outside, she examined the scratches with some pride. What a way to leave a mark.

She was just about to open the back door, when she heard a loud thud coming from behind the corner. It could have been nothing. Or it could have been an annoying sibling caught in the act of snooping.

Lucy started slowly walking towards the source of the noise. Then a familiar face appeared from behind a crate.

There he was: the idiot brother. His eyes wide open in a wild expression, he was waving at her to move closer.

She threw a glance at the hangar door to make sure it remained closed, no Skaara nor human watching, then she rushed to Frank, and pushed him further out of sight. "What the fuck are you doing here? I told you to stay away," she whispered as loudly as she dared, throwing a punch to his left arm to stress the point.

"Ow! Is it the space invader that told you to hit intruders? Or are you really that committed to the cause?" he protested.

"I was committed to the cause of keeping you alive, but I'm kind of changing my mind about that." She didn't mean that yet did nothing to fill the moment of silence that followed.

Frank was massaging his arm, his expression a mix of disappointment and hopelessness, a look she was very familiar with.

He didn't get it. That wasn't exactly a surprise, but she was sure she deserved better than that. He wasn't even trying to understand that she was trying to keep him out of that mess to save his life. Instead, he stared at her as if she was a lost cause – the reckless, ill-intentioned, naïve younger sister. She had heard all that before. Uncanny how Frank had grown up to be their father.

"Get out of here before he sees you," she hissed at him.

"Why are you still working for that thing?" he asked, his voice softer, which irritated Lucy even more.

She wasn't going to explain to him that *that thing* had developed the habit of threatening him anytime it needed a favour. She clenched her jaw and squared her feet. "I don't know how you got here, but you have to get out. Don't make me ask you again."

"I'm not going anywhere until that thing is destroyed."

"Now you're being dramatic."

"Luce, I'm going to blow it up."

She couldn't have heard that right. "You're going to do what now?"

Frank took off his backpack and opened it to reveal its contents – a couple of long square boxes, with wires and fuses sticking out of them. Lucy was not an expert, but she could guess those were the sort of boxes that went *boom*.

"Where did you even get this? And how did you bring it in here?"

"Matt knows a few people," he explained, and Lucy froze at the realisation. "To be honest, I prepared this without even knowing how to bring it in here, then he called me this morning, and guess what? He thought I was with you. Are you still surprised that I came to find you?"

Matthew knew she had lied to him. Great. One more thing she'd have to deal with, if she ever got out of there alive – which was becoming increasingly unlikely, by the way. "You're saying you figured out a bomb in less than twenty-four hours, graduated 007, then got Matthew to sneak you in here."

"I'm a chemistry student, remember? Making things go boom and fizz is kind of our thing."

"I thought making vodka out of potatoes was your thing."

"We do more than one thing," he replied quickly. "Are you going to help me or not?"

"You're not serious," she said. He couldn't be serious. It was utter madness. "I'm so definitely not going to help you. You're going to blow up an army camp. How are you even considering this? What is wrong with you?"

His eyes were wide and wild. He looked and sounded like a fanatic. "It needs to be done. Clearly the army has been infiltrated. This is bigger than we even realised. Someone has to get rid of that thing."

"Then let the soldiers do it. Call the lieutenant, or the colonel, or freaking Captain Britain if that's what it takes."

"Turns out, being possessed by an alien lowers your credibility scores," he said with a bitter smirk.

"Blowing things up is going to make you popular instead?" she shot back. "Use your fucking brain, Frankie. Get out of here and let me take care of this."

"That thing wants to take over the planet, Luce," he insisted. "I don't know what you think you'll get out of it, but you won't get it, I can tell you now. And even if you do, ask yourself, is it worth the whole of humanity? Is it, Luce?"

That big-brother sense of superiority was written all over his face. *Yes*, she wanted to tell him. *Yes, it's going to be worth it if it keeps us both alive.*

He wasn't really getting it, though. She glanced down at the explosive. His whole plan was to send things *ka-boom*. She was

FIRST ALIEN

the one who should have been disappointed. She who might actually have a chance to screw up the whole alien invasion from the inside, if she only figured out how. And she was being chastised for it. She loved her brother to bits, but not like that.

She wasn't going to persuade him to give up that madness, so there was only one thing left for her to do.

"Give me the backpack." He was hesitating, so Lucy explained, "You're right, I'm being selfish. This thing is dangerous, and we need to get rid of it. Also, you won't be able to get close enough to the spaceship without somebody seeing you, but I can."

"You are serious."

"I am, and I need you to trust me. I'm your sister, not an alien terrorist."

He still didn't look convinced.

That was when Cook made his appearance at the door. Whatever Lucy could have done to save Frank, it just went up in smoke.

Her brother shouldn't have been there. She had told him not to come. She had told him to stay away. He hadn't listened to her, so this one was on him. Yet somehow it felt a lot like Lucy's fault.

It took Frank a couple of seconds to realise something was wrong.

"Lucy, why don't you bring the bag inside," ordered Cook.

Reluctantly, Lucy did as she was told. Frank called out to her, but by then she was already closing the door between them.

She paused for a moment there. Her eyes burnt with tears, while she told herself Cook wouldn't kill him as long as he needed her – as long as she did what the Skaara asked her to do.

When she looked up, Stephanie was standing by the shelves, hugging the metal structure and trusting it to keep her upright. She was looking right at Lucy, as if she knew exactly what was going on.

Lucy averted eye contact and soldiered on. She was doing what she had to do.

That's the thing, Lucy told herself. *There's no other way.*

- XIV -

Stephanie was barely resisting the urge to sit. The nausea had gone, at least, and she didn't feel faint anymore.

It felt as if, whatever conditioning the Skaara had put on her, it was slowly fading, and now that she had conquered the upright position, she was itching to put the shooting to the test too.

There wasn't an actual plan yet. There was a chance Lucy was going to take care of Frank, but Stephanie couldn't count on her for anything else. As far as she knew, she was on her own, the weight of the whole planet on her shoulders.

A thorough search of the shelves and surrounding space had resulted in three loose screws and one split roofing nail hidden in the corner between the floor and the wall. None of those things could be helpful in getting her out of the handcuffs. She had tried the split nail, but only managed to tighten its grip around the metal support.

Looking at the structure, she counted the junctions and the screws. She could have slid the handcuffs out of the frame if she took some pieces apart. Alas, there wasn't a screwdriver in her inventory.

She had her house keys, though. She selected the thinnest one and tried it on the screw. First attempt, it slipped off the drive and almost flattened it. It was never going to work, and it would only make it worse.

Dropping the keys back in her pocket, she gazed wistfully at the nail, its head as large as a thimble. She moved her gaze to the screws. She tried it on. It fit the drive perfectly, and she barely suppressed a squeal. She wondered if carpenters ever got as excited about nail heads as she was getting just then.

Three more screws kept the bottom shelves tight to the support, and none of them were as loose as the first one. She set to work carefully and silently. She had to stop when Lucy and the Chief walked by on their way to visit the spacecraft and, since then, she had to keep an ear out for their chatter, lest either of the two walk in on her escape plan and make unwelcome adjustments.

After what felt like hours – it was barely minutes, really – she was about to tackle the next screw when the chatter stopped. Stephanie heard steps approaching, and she turned her back to cover the unscrewed side of the shelf.

Lucy wasn't interested in her, though, and headed straight out the door. If she was deliberately ignoring her, Stephanie didn't have time to care. She went back to work and managed to get to the last of the screws just as the Chief's steps announced his arrival.

The middle shelf had a corner visibly hanging loose. She stood up to face the door, keeping as still as she could and holding onto the frame, as if it would suddenly collapse. However, he walked right past her and out the door.

Stephanie certainly didn't miss the attention, yet it was starting to feel insulting how everybody was dismissing her so.

Seconds later, Lucy appeared. She was carrying a backpack, and there was something pained in her expression. Stephanie's heart skipped a beat in anticipation. *Frank*, she thought. *Something must have happened to him*.

With the backpack left leaning against the wall right in front of the open side of the spacecraft, Lucy walked back out, leaving the door ajar behind her. If she noticed the loosened shelf, she didn't say anything.

As for the backpack, it could have contained anything – something the Skaara needed for their invasion, or something Frank had brought to kill the beast. Either way, the alien had it now, and placed somewhere Stephanie couldn't get to without exposing herself, which would take her right back to square one.

Being almost free from the handcuffs was little consolation. She was cornered and outnumbered, watching Earth's invasion from a front row seat. To make things worse, the Skaara had earned a hostage.

The door closed with a jerk, and Stephanie was left in the buzzing silence of the hangar. Alone, if not for the alien in the spaceship.

She worked at the last screws and finally managed to pull them all off. Sliding the handcuffs off the shelving, however, was going to make some noise. Even if the Skaara wasn't paying attention – and it probably was – there was little chance Stephanie could escape unnoticed.

Leaning back against the wall, scars brushing against the fabric of her shirt, she winced at the lingering pain, then exhaled and let it hit her. For a second there, she thought she understood Lucy's choice.

The Skaara were always going to win. There was a whole spaceship full of them waiting to land. *Kill one, and they're only going to send more*. She wasn't fooling anyone. There was no point in fighting.

Maybe it was time to give up.

She closed her eyes and took a deep breath. Her shoulders felt heavy and tense. She wrapped her fingers around the cold metal of the handcuffs. She breathed out.

Fuck it, she thought. If dying was in the program, she was going to make it worth the ticket.

When she opened her eyes again, she was ready to move. She only had to figure out which way was best to go. It didn't take long. The back door was visible from the inside of the spaceship, and she was never going to make it without the Skaara grabbing at her and sending her to some nowhere place in the metaphorical boot of her mind. Whatever was in the backpack, she'd need to circle back, if she got the chance.

It had to be the front door.

She dropped the roofing nail in her pocket, then tried to create enough room between the metal bars of the shelves to slide the metal bracelet through, but the metallic creaking was so loud she had to stop. She couldn't do it. It wasn't going to work.

To hell with it. She grabbed her gun with her free hand, ready to empty the whole cartridge on the creature if it came at her. If she couldn't aim straight at it, maybe she would get lucky with a stray bullet.

Leveraging the shelf as far as she could from the metal frame, she managed to slide the handcuffs past the first shelf. The noise she made was jarring, yet it didn't seem to carry far enough for the Skaara to hear. Good to know some luck was going her way after all.

The most challenging part, however, was about to come. She placed herself in front of the shelving unit and gripped its foot with her free hand. The frame wasn't heavy, but it was dangerously unstable.

She only needed an inch, but the whole structure started to oscillate halfway up. She pinned her back against it to give support, and the sudden pain took her breath for a moment. Biting her lip, she pulled up the foot an inch further and swung her right arm up in the air, finally free.

"Yes," she whispered while a grin spread across her face, the pain almost forgotten already. Looking at her unbound hand felt like seeing it for the first time. Dramatic, she realised, but it had been a long day.

She could feel the blood flowing again, the adrenaline was rushing, and every new breath was full of potential. She moved her arm around, enjoying the freedom. Even the sore skin on her back didn't hurt as much anymore.

The alien was still working away on the other side of the ship. If she kept silent, there was a good chance she could make it to the front door without being caught.

No sound was coming from the back door. Lucy and Cook were likely still figuring out how to deal with the unwanted guest. Frank was going to be useful, after all, if only as a distraction.

Stephanie gripped the loose end of the handcuffs, holding the ring in a fist, ready to weaponize it, then tiptoed her way to the front of the door. Almost on the threshold, and the spaceship was still between her and the Skaara. The door, however, was a different kind of challenge.

She reluctantly slid the gun back in its holster.

She couldn't avoid the noise of the door opening and then closing; therefore, she had to count on her speed of execution.

Hands ready on the door handle, she counted to three in her mind. Then, cringing at the loud whirring of the hinges, she pulled the door open, stepped out, and let it slam behind her with a loud clang. No way the Skaara hadn't heard that.

Outside, the sun hit her eyes like a fireball. As she stepped away from the door, she lost her balance for a moment. Everything wobbled and shimmered around her. She closed her eyes and pressed herself against the warm metal behind her.

Then she listened. Compared to the muffled interior, the silence outside was full of a different kind of buzz. The camp was a hive of noises and voices, and birds chirping in the trees – they didn't care about the Skaara planning to take over the world, and Stephanie wished she could stop caring as well.

"You alright over there?" somebody asked her.

She opened her eyes again and straightened up, giving her best impression of a person in control of herself. "Of course," she said.

She was looking at two soldiers. The brainwashed one she had met in the morning, and the extra brain that should have been watching the back door.

"It's claustrophobic, isn't it?" the extra brain said. "Awfully narrow in there."

The other one smirked. "Don't know what I expected from you agency brats. Failed army recruit, aren't you? Couldn't handle the pressure? I bet that's why they called us in," he said, ending his contribution in an annoying cackle.

The first one – Gill, his name tag said – intervened, shoving the other one aside. "Stop being a dick, Scott. It's horrible when that happens. My sister used to get a panic attack every time she walked into an elevator. Going to visit our nan was seven flights of stairs every time."

Stephanie hadn't meant for that to be a conversation. The other soldier – Scott – was about to respond when she cut

FIRST ALIEN

him short. "That sounds awful, but I really should go check on something over there." She pointed vaguely at the side of the hangar, the one flanked by the perimeter fence. The two soldiers shrugged and lost interest as she walked away from them.

There were cameras pointing straight at her. It was only half past midday, so the pre-recorded loop should have still been playing in the security marquee, with Sergeant Marker keeping watch over an eventless space. Just in case it wasn't, however, she crossed her arms, hiding the loose handcuffs in the hollow of her elbow as she walked to the side of the building. She stopped shy of turning the corner.

There were a few metres between the hangar wall and the metallic fence. The ground was littered with empty crates and scraps of metal, with just enough room left for a van-sized vehicle to drive through. As ugly a sight as it was, it played in Stephanie's favour. She made her way between metal slates and crate corpses, easily managing to keep behind cover on most sides.

Bits of branches and fragments of wood were scattered on the beaten track that ran along the wall, probably a testimony of Lucy's driving skills.

When Stephanie finally caught sight of the girl and the Chief, they were standing by the far corner of the hangar. The van was parked right beside them, a huge scratch on its side, to confirm her assessment of Lucy's driving abilities.

Frank's limp body was lying on the ground in front of them.

It looked like they were in a heated conversation, although their voices didn't carry far enough for Stephanie to understand what they were saying.

They hadn't noticed her escape yet. That was odd. The Skaara

182

must have heard the door closing when she left. Maybe neither the alien nor the Chief thought her worth worrying about. It wasn't flattering, but Stephanie felt like being grateful for that small mercy.

To her right, against a young beech tree, she noticed a short pile of small crates that would offer the cover she needed while gaining sight of her target. She took the tranquiliser gun out of its holster and secured her grip. She had to be sure her arm and hand weren't going to fail her. She was going to take the shot this time.

She raised her weapon and steadied her elbow on a bit of wood jutting out from the skeleton crate. She breathed out and relaxed her shoulders, testing her aim on Lucy first. Then she shifted to target the Chief's chest, and that was when it started.

A sense of nausea first, then her hand started shaking. Even if she managed to pull the trigger, she wasn't going to hit the target if it had been as big as a hill. She might as well have shouted out at them to get out of the line of fire.

With her failing shooting abilities, her plan was feeling increasingly hopeless. She should have reached out, got the army to intervene and stop the invasion, because that was what the army was there to do.

On the other hand, it only took the sergeant intercepting her, and all her credibility would be shoved down the drain, and with it the only chance to prevent the worst from happening. Not to mention, she knew how soldiers felt about private agencies working on their turf – she had just had a snarky demonstration of it.

Stephanie was still considering her limited options when the Chief stalked off and went back into the hangar.

"Shit," she whispered, cowering behind the tree. Right when

she thought things couldn't get any worse. *He's going to come after me*, she thought.

Meanwhile, Lucy had turned her back to her, and it looked as if she was tending her brother – except she wasn't, unless searching through his pockets was meant to be a caring practice.

In a matter of seconds, the Chief was walking back out, carrying with him one of those pods he had shown her. Instead of loading it onto the van, however, he called Lucy near him to tell her something, then walked off in the opposite direction and out of sight.

Whatever was going through Lucy's head, Stephanie didn't have time to find out. The Chief's disinterest, as insulting as it could be, was giving her a small window of breath. She was going to use it to give the Skaara some human spirit to chew on, in the hope that its whole species would choke on it.

She was ready to leave her hiding place when Lucy turned to gaze around at the desolation of fenced trees and empty crates. She was looking for her, Stephanie was sure. Gun at the ready, she walked out.

Let's do this, then.

- XV -

It was just a tranquilising gun, Cook had said. He was a man of his word, he had said. Also, no use in having dead bodies lying around, when living hostages were so much more useful.

There was a lot that Lucy hadn't liked about that. If she had to be honest with herself, she didn't like Cook's plan for Davis either, but she was a big girl and a trained assassin or something, so she could get herself out of it on her own.

Her brother was something else. Yes, he could be a patronising idiot, and yes, he had walked himself into that place – carrying explosives, nonetheless – but he was *her* explosive-carrying idiot. If anybody had a right to shoot him with Xanax, that was her, not a brainwashed alien puppet.

As far as she could see, Frank's breathing was regular. She pressed a hand against his chest and felt his heart beating. It seemed slow, but it was still ticking at least.

The instruction was to leave him there, get the pods to the van, and drive out of camp, destination to be confirmed. Lucy considered the positioning of the van. A skilled driver would have no problem staying clear of him. The graveyard of splintered wood she left behind her when driving the van there, however, put her somewhere below being the best driver in the world.

185

She had to move him away, somewhere to the side, maybe even leaning against the wall – maybe even inside the van, so she could take him away with her and out of danger. The simple movement of kneeling beside him, however, sent daggers up her lower back. "If I ever get out of this, I'm dedicating my life to yoga," she murmured to herself.

She took a moment to breathe while the pins of pain subsided. She felt in her pocket for the pink sloth. She wasn't sure what she was hoping to achieve that way, but she stuffed it in Frank's pocket anyway. Maybe what was in the flash drive could give him some idea that didn't involve explosives – or it could end up right back in Cook's hands, with the Skaara recognising the plush toy and spelling her doom. She had to get Frank and the sloth out of there.

The explosives. She hadn't meant to mention anything to Cook, but he had yanked the backpack out of her hands. He had sniggered when he had realised what it was, then told her to bring it inside. It might be useful later, he had said, before trusting her with a bag full of explosives. Oddly reassuring.

The back door opened behind her, and she perked up to see Cook walk out. He was carrying one of the pods with him and was clearly trying to stay out of sight. He waved at her to walk over, so she did.

"Leave him there and move the pods. You need to get out of here as soon as possible," he said, glancing around as if afraid something was going to jump at him from behind a crate.

"Why? I thought we had until four."

He moved further away from the corner of the hangar and lowered his voice. "Davis has found a way out. Make sure you lock the van anytime you get back inside."

"Why would she come for the van? She's got a motorcycle

out front."

"She might be hanging around here to play hero. Gwyn will keep a feeler for the pods. You watch out and complete the job."

None of that felt reassuring. "What if I find her first, instead? Shoot her with the sleepy gun or something?" she asked, but Cook had already turned the other way. Of course, he was never going to fall for that.

"She's irrelevant. The pods are priority. Get a move on, human."

He walked away before Lucy could say anything else. He hadn't mentioned the backpack, nor the explosives. It was possible Davis had overlooked that as well – she couldn't have guessed what was inside, anyway.

She glanced down at Frank. He needed moving onto the van, and the pods had to be loaded right next to him. Then the backpack, because she wasn't going to leave that behind. She had no time to linger, yet she couldn't shake the feeling that someone was watching her.

Cook had seemed sure Davis was going to play hero, yet it was just as possible she'd try to raise the whole camp against them. Lucy could almost picture her explaining to the major – or the captain or whatever – how the space crawlers were going to invade Earth, and they had to stop the Evil Alien Mastermind before it was too late. She could also picture the whole army camp laughing at her.

No, that couldn't be what Davis had in mind. By then, she had a personal stake in that. She was going to take care of it herself.

She turned to survey the littered ground between the hangar and the perimeter fence. There were enough hiding spots to conceal a small army.

Getting out of there with Frank and the pods was the main priority, she reminded herself, yet she couldn't help looking, part of her almost wishing Davis would appear from behind one of the trees. Then, as if coming straight out of her imagination, she did.

Lucy had to resist the urge to pinch herself. Instead, she glanced sideways, to make sure Cook was out of sight. He had turned the corner already, for however long he was going to stay there.

Once again, Davis was pointing a gun at her, and whether it was a real or a sleepy one was largely irrelevant. Lucy showed her empty hands and started walking towards her. They were only a few feet apart when she opened her mouth to say something – a joke, or a greeting, she hadn't figured out that part yet.

Davis wasn't in a joking mood, though. "Not another step."

Still as a statue, her arms still raised as high as her shoulders, Lucy tried again, "I just wanted to ..."

"Don't," Davis cautioned her, stepping closer.

So dramatic. Lucy gestured zipping her mouth closed, then held both arms a bit higher than before. She couldn't say she felt threatened. If Davis hadn't shot her before, Lucy was sure she wasn't going to shoot her then either.

"What happened to your brother?"

Lucy kept her lips shut tight. She was vaguely aware that pulling an attitude could be counterproductive. She also didn't care. It took a couple of seconds for Davis to catch up with the joke.

"Seriously? How old are you?"

Lucy shrugged and dropped her arms. "Old enough to drink, if that's your fancy."

"What happened to Frank?"

Davis hadn't liked the joke, clearly. *Some people lack a critical sense of humour*, thought Lucy, then exhaled and said, "Your boss shot him."

"You seem very calm about it."

She was terrified. Good to know her poker face was holding up. "It was a sleepy gun," explained Lucy. "Just like yours."

That was a wild assumption, an attempt to understand what kind of life-threatening risk she was staring at. Ignoring the comment, Davis took another step forward. The gun – a sleepy one, she was sure now, was within Lucy's reach. She considered reaching for it, then remembered how poorly it went the last time she had tried that.

"I need you to tell me the Skaara's plan," Davis was saying. "We can still stop this thing, save your brother, get out of here without a space lizard crawling on our backs."

"Do you always ask for help while aiming a gun at people?"

"Not the first time," admitted Davis.

"How did it work for you in the past?"

"Mixed results."

"Have you considered saying *please*?"

"Did you become a pacifist before or after agreeing to cooperate in an alien invasion?"

Touché. She wasn't going to convince Davis to lay down her weapon that way. Telling the truth was maybe worth a try. "Listen, I'm not enjoying this either, you know? Watching my brother get shot? Not the highlight of my day. Spending my time with a mind-controlled arsehole, not my favourite. But guess what? There's no other way."

The gun was still steady and aimed at her, but Davis had at least flinched at her sudden openness. Lucy went on, "Think

189

about it, if these space crawlers have the power and technology to travel all the way here, what chance do we have against them?"

Davis' face was unreadable. "We have to try."

That was exasperating. She should have caught on already. There was no winning.

"Sometimes there are fights you can't win," Lucy said, resenting how much her tone sounded like Frank's. "Sometimes, the only chance you get is if you hold on tight and do your best to survive."

"Is that what you do?" replied Davis, her upper lip curled into a grimace. "Is that what you think you're doing here? Just holding on tight? Doing your best? Tell me, how many people are going to die while you do that?"

"So what? You think that blowing up one spaceship is going to save the planet? News flash, it won't. Kill one, they'll send another, maybe ten others, and what are you going to do then?"

Shit. That was a lot of things she hadn't meant to say. A lot of things that terrified her. She clenched her fists to stop her hands from trembling.

Something lit up in Davis' expression. "That's what's in the backpack then. Your brother wanted to blow up the spaceship, is that it?"

That could not have gone worse. Lucy held her tongue.

"I'll take that as a yes."

"That's not what I said."

"Drop the act, Campbell. You're not as good at this as you think you are."

Lucy recoiled. That wasn't fair. She didn't deserve that. "And you stop living in a fucking action film. What do you want me to say? That my brother brought dynamite in here? Yes, he did, and he was going to blow up the whole thing, and probably me, you, and himself in the process. While all I wanted was to save his sorry ass. But hey, come and point your gun at me, while Frankie's the hero, right? Never mind his plan was fit for low-level terrorism. Tell me, how am I still the bad guy here?"

She regretted saying every word as soon as it flew out of her mouth. Her eyes were stinging as tears gathered, so she swallowed the wave of sobs that had collected in her throat. At least she had managed to keep her voice down.

"You're right," said Davis a moment later, then slowly lowered the gun. "It was a stupid idea. He didn't consider a lot of things, but he did get one thing right."

Lucy scoffed. "You're still going to blow up the spaceship."

"Not until you and your brother are safely out of here," replied Davis. Her voice was growing softer.

Lucy wondered if that was the sort of thing they taught as a conflict resolution technique. She wanted to snap back at her, but her pot of sarcasm was suddenly empty. She was scared for Frank, as well as for herself. "Do you really think you can pull this off?"

If Davis had a way out, it couldn't be such a bad idea to see how far she could go. Too bad she wasn't answering the question. *Of course*, Lucy thought. "You're full of shit, just like everyone else."

There wasn't time for Stephanie to respond. Lucy lashed forward, charging shoulder first against Davis' chest, while trying to wrestle the gun out of her hand, hoping the surprise would be enough to give her the upper hand. She quickly realised it wasn't.

The reaction was a flash. Lucy wasn't even sure how she ended up with her arm behind her back, locked once again in a chokehold that left no space for air nor for wondering how far Davis was willing to take it. She could barely move her upper body. As for the gun, it was pressing uncomfortably against the soft spot behind her ear.

A second later, the hold around her neck loosened just enough for her to catch her breath. She was faintly aware of Davis' voice in her ear. "Don't make me do this."

"Why not?" managed Lucy. "Wouldn't it be easier that way?"

"There's easy, and there's right."

What a pile of rubbish. As if Davis was sorry about what she was doing. As if someone – or something – was forcing her to act that way. No, that excuse had left and crawled into the spaceship hours before.

"Bullshit," she replied. What was right for some people always ended up being wrong for everybody else. The *right thing* was as much of a myth as the yeti was.

"Maybe," conceded Davis, to Lucy's surprise. "But I'm going to do it anyway, and you either help me set this right, or I'll have to force you out of my way."

There was a pause, as if the entire wood was waiting for Lucy to say something. She didn't.

"It's like you said," Davis continued, "some battles you can't win, so take your brother, take the van, and get out of here."

Just like that, Lucy couldn't hold on anymore. Her shoulders started trembling and tears were streaming down her cheeks. She didn't know what to do. Crying was not the strategy she had chosen, yet she just couldn't help it.

She barely realised Davis had slowly lowered the gun and let go of her. As Lucy's knees went weak, both women sunk to the ground. This time, Davis' hold around her was of a different kind. She took a couple of deep breaths, conscious she had to get a grip, while at the same time wishing she could sit there for the rest of her life. The release of tension had left her empty of all her strength.

"We have to move away from here," said Davis softly in her ear. "We can't let the Chief see me. Can you stand?"

Lucy had no idea if she could. She nodded anyway, then surprised herself with rising on both feet, albeit hanging tight onto Davis' shoulder. She was breathing normally again, and the world looked brighter for it.

In that moment of clarity, it felt important to let Davis know. "I just wanted to keep Frank safe," she said.

"I know," Davis replied, looking at her with some concern. "Will you be able to drive out of here?"

There was even half a smile when Lucy replied, "I guess I'm not national threat number one anymore."

Davis went all dark then and replied, "Let's be clear, if I see you talking to Cook, I'm shooting you on the spot." Even then, her tone wasn't half as hard as her words. She turned to the van. "Let's load the bomb guy quickly onto the van, unless you want to explode together with the Skaara in there."

"Nope, I like my limbs attached," teased Lucy, letting go of her support and starting off towards her brother.

"Of course, you do," murmured Davis.

There was some heaviness in her tone. Lucy hadn't yet stopped to think how hard the last couple of days must have been for the agent, but the signs were all over her face and voice. At least it sounded like the Skaara hadn't succeeded in turning her brain to mush.

Davis glanced down at Frank with a pained expression that Lucy didn't know how to interpret. The loose handcuff was hanging by her side. "You grab the shoulders, and I'll get the legs," she said.

"Hold on."

Lucy had kept the small key in her pocket, waiting for the opportunity to slip it to Davis. She produced it then and handed it to her. "I managed to slip my hand in his pocket."

Davis nodded, then offered her wrist. "I'm not left-handed."

"I was going to give them to you, before I went," she explained.

"Campbell, we don't have time for this," she interrupted. "Grab his shoulders, and I'll get the legs."

Even sharing the load, Frank was a heavy cargo to shift around. Bracing herself, Lucy grabbed Frank's shoulder and did her best to ignore the pain in her back. They managed to sit him on the floor of the van, then drag him all the way in. He didn't even stir. The sleepy bullet was going to keep him down for hours, she had been told. She couldn't help worrying if he was going to stay unconscious for longer – or maybe forever.

As she was closing the door of the van on him, Davis stepped away towards the back door of the hangar. She seemed ready to pounce straight at the Skaara. If that was her plan, she was going to get herself killed. "You'll have to get the space crawler out of there before you pull your hero stunt," Lucy told her.

Davis didn't turn when she shot back, "I'm sorry, are you telling me how to do my job?"

The sarcasm wasn't enough to hide the tension in her tone. Davis knew she wasn't going to get out of there alive – at least not without help.

"I can get the space crawler out of there," Lucy offered. "Buy you a bit of time, so you can set up the explosives."

Turning to face her, Davis didn't look so convinced. "If it notices that you're leaving camp, it might hook onto the van. I can't let it get out of here."

"Out of here on its own is better than in here hooked on your brain, don't you think? That thing is going to get you as soon as you step in there. Do you want to sit here and make a list of pros and cons, or do you want to blow up the invasion plan?"

Davis conceded with a nod. "How are you going to get it out?"

There was an oak tree not far from the corner of the hangar, inside the perimeter fence and only a few steps from the door. Lucy raised the handcuffs to show her weapon, then waved at the tree. "Go hide behind there and let me take care of it."

As soon as Davis was out of sight, Lucy walked to the back door, opened it a sliver and stuck her hand inside, banging the handcuffs against the wall. "Help!" she shouted through the opening. "Can I have some fucking help over here? I'm being attacked, you star-born arsehole!"

It was the loudest sound she dared to make – hopefully, the spaceship noise-cancelling effect was enough to prevent the rest of the army from hearing it. She glanced nervously in the distance, yet nobody seemed to have taken any notice. Maybe she hadn't screamed loud enough, considering the Skaara hadn't bothered showing its ugly face either.

She took a breath and was about to resume her banging when the space crawler finally showed itself at the door, its movement visibly more frantic than usual, surveying the ground around the van. Lucy thought it looked panicked.

She waved her hands and pointed at the pathway along the side of the hangar. "She ran that way, took the van keys with her. Hurry, or she'll get Captain Britain to come here before you know it," she said, and the Skaara started moving away, following her directions.

So much for being a superior alien intelligence. Before the

crawler could figure out it had been played, Lucy jumped in the van, locked the doors, and started the engine.

She glanced around, but both Stephanie and the Skaara had disappeared from view. She switched to reverse gear, turned the van around and smashed a couple of crates in the process, then drove to the exit as fast as she could.

- XVI -

Sneaking into the narrow space of the hangar, the heaviness of the space hit her like a brick. Stephanie fought the waves of discomfort that still threatened to turn into a panic attack.

No time for that.

The Skaara was going to figure out that Lucy's cry for help was only a ruse, while the Chief was probably on his way back already.

The backpack was still where Lucy had left it. Inside were three packages, each one with a short fuse snaking out of a corner. It was a rudimentary way of making explosives, but still very stable and very effective. She could only guess at the composition, but she could trust a chemist to bake something strong enough to blow up a spaceship.

She found the box of matches in the external pocket. That was all she needed for showtime.

The odd shade of purplish light was still coming out of the side of the spaceship – in the rush to help Lucy, the Skaara had left the door open. It must have panicked.

How odd, thought Stephanie. All the time it had spent in her head, it had never felt like the kind of creature that would panic like that.

She pushed the thought aside, then grabbed the backpack

and headed inside. The pods were still lined up on the floor, close together in a sort of huddle, like so many eggs laid in a metallic space nest.

The walls of the hull were covered in pipes and grips, useful holds for the Skaara to navigate. Stephanie could almost picture it moving around, visiting nooks and crannies to check the ship systems. It was the most fascinating thing she had ever seen – and she was about to blow it all to pieces.

She took a deep breath, the odd alien scent filling the air with a dense electricity. She had to focus on the mission, the one where she was going to save the planet.

If she could find the fuel tank, that would make for a spectacular fire show. Alas, Stephanie had no idea where to look for it, and it was probably safer that way. She didn't want to blow up the whole forest if she could help it. The only thing that mattered was making sure that everything that was still inside the spaceship was destroyed.

One of the charges went in between the pods, while the other two she placed in opposite corners of the hull. With fire on all sides, there was little chance anything would survive.

She struck a match. It burned a blue flame for a moment, before turning pink. That wasn't something she was used to. Whatever she was breathing, it definitely wasn't oxygen.

The fuses looked long enough to give her enough time to get away. Hopefully not long enough for the Chief to find the charges and throw them out. She'd have to stall him to make sure.

She rushed outside. The coast seemed clear.

The van had disappeared, and there was no sign of the Skaara. If it had got onto the van and sneaked out of the camp, the space crawler was soon going to be stranded without a spaceship. If it was still around, there was a good chance it would turn into space barbecue. Not awful odds, Stephanie decided.

The next thing on her list was finding the Chief. She wasn't sure she would be able to shoot him, but she wasn't going to leave without trying, and she wouldn't have to wait long for that either.

When he appeared from behind the corner, Stephanie lifted her weapon and focused her attention on a spot just over the Chief's shoulder. Her arm was steady and her mind clear. So far so good.

He had come prepared too, and Stephanie recognised the gun in his hand as the one he had taken from her – the killing kind.

He smiled as he made his way to her. He didn't seem surprised to see her. "Aren't you tired of playing hero, Agent Davis?"

Enough of those games. "You shoot me, and you won't know where I hid the explosives," she told him.

"Stop trying to be smart," he replied. "There's only one place you would have placed them, isn't there?"

He was right. She wasn't in a place to negotiate. Good thing she only had to buy some time. "We both know I'm not the smart one. Still, I'd find some cover if I were you," she replied, sending a silent prayer to the explosives, to go off right then, even if it meant her blowing up with everything else.

The Chief wasn't moving, and he wasn't shooting. She didn't understand what he was waiting for.

Then it dawned on her.

She could picture the crawler coming up behind her.

She glanced at the tranquiliser gun. Benzodiazepine bullets. There was something the science team had told her about Skaara and benzodiazepines. They did not mix well.

She took a breath, closed her eyes, and turned the gun on

herself.

She pulled the trigger.

The world paused, the seconds chasing each other in anticipation, before the world exploded around them.

The noises had stopped somewhere on the way to the exit, but that did nothing to reassure Lucy. The space crawler could have been sitting quietly somewhere in the van, biding its time until she had to stop.

The Skaara had figured out the trick even before she had turned on the engine. It had thrown itself onto the windshield and clung to the wipers when she had tried to brush it off. It was only when she bumped into another one of the crates that the creature lost its grip and went flying straight to the ground.

Lucy hadn't lost any time wondering where it went. She had stepped on the gas, hoping she'd get past security before anyone could notice it wasn't an angry squirrel that was attacking her.

The gate was already in sight, when something hit the side of the van, then the passenger's window. Lucy cursed under her breath and kept on going.

That was the last she heard from the space crawler. By the time she had pulled up by the security cabin, all had gone quiet.

The soldier glanced at her pass and checked the schedule. Lucy was jittering. She knew the van inspection had been taken off the security's to-do list – Cook had made sure of that – and she was expected to leave the premises around that time anyway.

Even so, the soldiers didn't look too keen on letting her go that easily.

One of them knocked on the driver's window and asked her to lower it. "Name and purpose of your visit, miss?"

Lucy cringed at the miss-calling. "I'm here on Edward Cook's request. Check your notes. I have clearance to leave."

"Miss, I will need you to state your name. Can I see your pass?" he insisted.

"Call me *miss* one more time," she challenged him, half-wishing the Skaara would come out of its hiding place and grab hold of him right at that moment. She regretted the thought as soon as it came to her mind.

She could see he was about to tell her to step out of the van, when a cotton-haired woman came to her aid. It was a face she had seen before. "Lieutenant! It's such a relief to see a good soldier at work," she enthused. "This van, however, is authorised to go. I have the paperwork here."

She produced a document for the lieutenant to examine.

"Ma'am, with all due respect, we don't have ID on the driver. She refuses to state her name, and she hasn't produced her pass."

That was all Lucy could hear before they moved too far for the words to carry. When the soldier came back, he waved everyone else away, opened the gate and gestured for her to drive on.

Lucy was too relieved to wonder what had just happened. Once past the barrier, she pushed the van as fast as she could manage along the track.

Seconds later, she thought she heard an explosion somewhere in the distance. She glanced at the rear-view mirror once, then kept on going. She couldn't see anything through the trees, anyway.

As the track snaked through the woods and trees shifted beside her, Lucy shuddered at each bump in the road. She imagined the space crawler holding on to the underside of the van, waiting for her to stop. She couldn't drive forever, and she couldn't hide inside the vehicle for long either. That was what the woman in *Cujo* must have felt like.

If the Skaara had survived clinging to the van and riding with her out of the camp, she was toast. Unless she could turn the whole thing around. After all, there had been an explosion. She could claim she had provided the Skaara with the only way out of danger. Yes, that was a bulletproof reason, she decided. If the space crawler had survived, it was all thanks to her, so it better be grateful and not turn her brain into liquified grey matter.

Another glance in the rear-view mirror, and still no one following.

It was also possible the space crawler had stayed behind, gone back to the pods, and gotten caught in the explosion. A comforting thought, although Lucy couldn't quite bring herself to believe that.

Then there was Frank to deal with. He had spoken to Matthew, figured out what she was up to, and had shown up at the army camp on his own. He had brought explosives and, if she hadn't been around to stop him, he would have blown himself up, and he would've felt good about it too. He was probably going to expect a medal when he woke up.

With the spaceship blown to pieces, he *had* to finally let the whole thing go. She was going to send him off back to his life of vodka and glass beakers, and she'd make sure he never heard another word about the space crawler.

Slowly, she felt the tension release. Her arms relaxed on

the steering wheel, and she readjusted her weight on the seat, realigning her spine and softening her shoulders. There was no immediate danger. Everything was going to be fine. She was going to survive, and Frank was going to be fine too. That was all that mattered.

When she turned onto the main road, she finally caught her breath and relaxed into a moderate cruise speed. Still no sounds coming from below her feet, nor from behind her. It was tempting to think the Skaara was gone. So tempting – and so dangerous.

Once she had put a few more miles between her and the camp, Lucy pulled over and sat still for a moment, half expecting something to jump out of the glove compartment. Nothing did. She kept the engine running as a sort of deterrent. That would've been the perfect opportunity to look around the van for any Skaara stowaway, but she wasn't in a hurry to face the space crawler.

She searched her pockets for her phone instead. Her fingers brushed against the black box. It was still with her – it had been the whole day. She took it out and for a moment contemplated that mysterious and inaccessible black box. Something to figure out later.

First, there was a more pressing issue to resolve.

Matthew's phone rang twice before he answered. "Luce, what the hell is happening? How's Frankie?"

Such irony to that question. Funny thing was, she wasn't going to have to lie about it. "He's not in top shape, but nothing a few hours of sleep won't fix. Can you pick us up?"

"Yeah, of course. Just tell me you're not in trouble or anything."

"I'll explain later. Just come pick us up, okay?"

A short pause, then his voice again through the speaker. "Right. Okay. Meet you where I dropped you off?"

"Actually, do you remember where we went for that hike? The one where we had our encounter of the third kind?"

There was a moment of silence on the call. Lucy glanced around the space, wishing she could resume the driving.

Matthew was taking his dear time with his answer. He clearly wasn't too happy about the mention. If he had decided to stop helping her, that was a very shitty moment to do that.

"Mattie, are you still there?"

"There's a pub at the end of the trail, the Smoke and Mirrors," he said eventually. "That's where we were going to stop at the end of the hike."

Lucy put the call on speaker and opened the Google Maps. She wanted to end the call, but Matthew was still talking.

"Are you going to tell me why you went back there? And how did you get in there, anyway? Isn't the army controlling the place?"

"It's a long story," she interjected before he could go on asking pointless questions. "I'll tell you all you need to know while you buy me a drink. Now I've got to go. See you in a minute."

She ended the call as he tried to protest. She exhaled, bending her ear to the relative silence of the van. No weird sounds from anywhere around her. She located the pub on the map. It was only a few miles away and the only one in the area. It would take her seven minutes to get there.

She set the course and resumed driving.

* * *

The car park was as fancy as a small patch of dirt behind a repurposed farmhouse. It was somewhat reassuring to see only one other car there.

When Lucy opened the door of the van to get out, she paused for a moment, almost surprised that no space crawler had jumped on her yet.

She noticed the air around her, surprisingly fresh in the tepid November sun. The ground had already dried up after the previous day's rain, and the breeze was picking up the dust just enough to prompt a sneeze. She sniffed it away.

Looking in the general direction of the woods, she could see a pile of smoke bookmarking the spot where the spaceship had landed. She wondered if Davis had made it out before the blast. It was possible she had managed to survive. Heavily bruised and slightly singed, but still alive, nonetheless. Lucy made a mental note to look her up, maybe even visit her at the hospital.

She shook her head as she dismissed the thought. Wishful thinking, that was. Davis couldn't have survived, no matter how great a hero she managed to be.

Turning to the van, Lucy felt a twist in her gut. She walked around and even lifted herself up using the front seat as a step so that she could check the roof of the vehicle. As far as she could see, there was no space crawler anywhere in sight.

The underside, however, required a bit more courage than she could muster. Lucy hated the idea of sticking her head under the van, with the risk of coming face to face with the wretched creature.

She opened the back door and watched Frank still sleeping in there. She didn't step inside. Instead, she went to sit on the ground a few feet away.

If the Skaara had really been dangling beneath the van, or

hiding in the back with Frank, then it was going to come looking for her eventually. Lucy wrapped herself in her jacket, blaming the wind for the sudden chill.

With Frank still out cold for a few more hours, it was just her and the space crawler. "I'm going to give you five minutes, ugly space face," she said out loud. She then set a timer on her phone and placed it in front of her, watching the seconds tick away.

Five minutes was going to be plenty of time for the Skaara to get out. It was also plenty of time for Lucy's mind to wander to all sorts of places.

She took the small black box out of her jacket once again. It fit neatly in the palm of her hand, charcoal black and smooth to the touch. Even in the light of day, it looked like an uncomfortable spot of darkness.

Whatever it was, she didn't want it. She was going to give it back to Matthew, she decided – whatever he and his family had going on with it – and that was to be the end of it. The alien-invasion chapter of her life was on its last page. The timer counted down to one minute. She put the box back in her pocket. Everything in and around the van was still. Even the wind had quieted.

Thirty seconds, and nothing moved. She took a deep breath, held it for as long as she could, then exhaled, as if she could let out everything that had happened in the last three weeks. Maybe it really was that easy.

Three.

Two.

One.

Lucy picked up her phone and headed into the pub.

Acknowledgements

Not gonna lie, this is my baby and I'm supremely proud of myself for creating this. Yet, I could not have made it this far without the help and support of a number of people.

A huge thank you goes to Jerry Holliday and Bonafide Publishing, for listening to my rambling about alien spaceships and weird little monsters, for keeping me well caffeinated on our work days, and for believing that what was a half-baked idea for a story could become a full-fledged novel.

To my editor, Clara Abigail, goes my admiration and thanks. At times I thought she understood my story better than I did. There's plenty of editors out there, but I am most grateful it was her I happened to work with.

Thank you to the people who took the time to read this book when it was still an ugly duckling in desperate search for attention. They endured the worst of it, and saw the potential hidden beneath the rough surface. Rosy, Jordan, and Robin, I hope I lived up to your expectations. Thank you.

Writing can be a lonely business, so I consider myself blessed to be part of the most resilient group of scribblers Bristol had to give. We made it together through high and low tides, freezing winters and pandemics, picnics in the park and hilarious game nights. I met you by accident, and you became my family.

Special mention to my Libramica, soul-sister and occasional unwarranted therapist. I learned a lot about myself while writing this book, and a lot of it was thanks to our conversations. I am forever grateful for the time we spent together.

To friends close by and far away, those that sat with me at my most vulnerable, and laughed with me at my brightest – thank you. You know who you are, and I love you all.

I wouldn't have gotten this far without my family. My sister made me who I am, and so to her goes my biggest thank you. *Ti voglio bene, Fra.*

Join Maddie Marzola's Reading Group

Click here to join **Maddie Marzola's Reading Group and newsletter** and get a free eBook download of The First Landing. head over to:

www.maddiemarzola.com

Please also consider leaving a review where you purchased this book. It's hugely appreciated. Thank you!

About the Author

Maddie Marzola has been many things before becoming a writer - English tutor, science graduate, barista, football player, and ice cream vendor. Nowadays, she splits herself between an ordinary 9-to-5 clerical job and an extraordinary 5-to-9 writing life. Allowing for some sleep in between.

Science-Fiction is by far her favourite playground - a fascinating world of endless possibilities, a blank canvas where to paint wild scenarios and impossible dreams. Not all of these make it into her books, but there's fun in trying.

The UK has been home for most of her adult life, and she found her writing family in Bristol.

Ingram Content Group UK Ltd.
Milton Keynes UK
UKHW040107130523
421680UK00001B/59

9 781916 239739